True North:
<u>Not</u> Strong
and Free

True North:
Not Strong
and Free

Defending the
Peaceable Kingdom
in the Nuclear Age

Peter C. Newman

McClelland and Stewart

McClelland and Stewart Limited
The Canadian Publishers
25 Hollinger Road
Toronto, Ontario
M4B 3G2

Canadian Cataloguing in Publication Data
Newman, Peter C., 1929-
  True north: not strong and free

ISBN 0-7710-6798-4

1. Canada — Defenses. I. Title.

| UA600.N4 | 355'.033071 | C83-098762-2 |

Printed and bound in Canada by
T. H. Best Printing Company Limited

In affectionate memory of my friend and fellow sailor,
William Strange (1902-1983).

BY THE SAME AUTHOR:

Peace is brief,
as fragile and transitory
as apple blossoms in the spring.

—Barbara Tuchman

Contents

Foreword

THIS SMALL BOOK ON A BIG SUBJECT is an attempt by a concerned journalist to examine, in a fairly critical way, Canada's current defence posture – which hovers precariously close to a pratfall.

The problems are military; their solutions must be political. The trouble is that our parliamentary system tends to isolate our defence strategists. Civilian control of the military in any democracy is essential. But the politicians cannot have it both ways: if they want to claim responsibility for Canadian defence, they must assume the leadership required on the issue. They haven't.

Merely throwing inadequate funds at defence department officials and expecting them to muddle through somehow is not enough – especially since the alternative is to surrender our sovereignty to one of the two superpowers that happen to be our neighbours.

In this uneasy autumn of 1983, national defence has become a subject considered worth debating, largely because of public controversy over the Trudeau government's agreement to test the American cruise missile. That is an essential part of a range of questions examined in this book – but it's only a part. The cruise debate should not be allowed to curtail or derail the much more significant arguments over Canada's overall defence policy, or the lack of it.

This book is dedicated to that wider debate.

THE PROBLEM IN DEALING with anything as emotional as defence is that what people lack in evidence, they often make up for in conviction – adamantly-held conclusions are often drawn on the basis of shaky data. Thus we have a growing populist disarmament movement – solidly rooted in the Canadian tradition of liberal

11

humanism – rejecting the notion of deterrence and advocating instead the unilateral dismantling of Canada's (and the West's) defences. Its advocates are convinced that the military choices open to Canada have become the equivalent of municipal zoning issues, with all the big decisions being made "downtown" – in Washington and Moscow.

That may be true, but any country that hands over holus-bolus the ability to defend itself to any other country automatically becomes that parent-nation's colony. This is a fate against which many Canadians, myself among them, have fought in both the economic and cultural arenas. It need not happen.

In this book I have concentrated on dissecting our current defence establishment and examining some options.

Canadian politicians during the past three decades – and both major parties are equally guilty, the Liberals more so only because they have been in power longer – have perpetuated fraud on a grand scale. It is nothing short of a criminal act for the politicians to pretend that our warriors, clad in uniforms the colour and style of green garbage bags, are adequately equipped to defend themselves, much less to guard the nation, or even any province, county, or town.

But blaming the politicians is a mug's game. It may be a thought beyond endurance, but, like most democracies, we get the politicians we deserve, and their actions pretty well reflect our moods. Ottawa's inability to mobilize any national resolve has left us short-changed in adequate military potential, defence of our economic sovereignty, protection of our environment, and the nurturing of our cultures. Our politicians have unfortunately reflected accurately the psychology of surrender that pervades our national character.

The conquest of any nation rarely takes place on the battlefield, or even in business boardrooms. It occurs within the soul of a people and in the minds of their leaders. Colonization requires two participants; conquest implies a surrender. This rush to mental abdication, so prevalent in our history, is dictated not by population size or by any other economic factors. It is rooted in the disconcerting concept that something is lacking within us which a more powerful and determined outsider may be able to provide.

I reject such a garrison mentality.

12

My hope is that this study will invigorate the existing dialogue on defence priorities and ways to establish them, particularly at a time when both the critics and servants of our military establishment agree there is something very wrong with the way we are dispensing our defence dollars – $30 billion is to be spent between 1983 and 1985.

Our forces will always be limited by their all-volunteer character. But that has not stopped us from making effective contributions to the defence of freedom during two world wars as well as participating in regional conflicts in such diverse parts of the globe as South Africa and Korea. The conflict over the Falkland Islands demonstrated that international honour can still be defended, even in this nuclear age, but the American misadventure in Vietnam and the Soviet invasion of Afghanistan proved that the defence of honour is not the only prerequisite of war.

I have not ever taken up arms on anyone's behalf, and, apart from my sporadic association with Canada's naval reserves (based much less on ideology than on my affinity for the sea), I am not a military man. But I do believe this country is worth defending and that no one else can do the whole job for us. Perhaps this book will prompt interested Canadians to start thinking in new directions.

I hope so.

CHAPTER ONE

Between the Eagle
and the Bear

*"There is little use in passing resolutions on vegetarianism
when the wolves are of another opinion."*
O. A. HOPKINS, CANADIAN FORCES CHAPLAIN

SOMEWHERE BETWEEN THE dread of the nuclear disarmers
and the paranoia of the warhawks, Canadians must find a
sensible defence policy to deal with the escalating threat to
peace.

The immutable forces of geography have made Canada a mus-
keg-moat over which the confrontation between superpowers will
be fought. We live directly under the trajectory of their atomic
armouries. The possibility of a nuclear firestorm hovers over both
our southern and northern horizons.

At the moment, much of our military spending is misdirected
and ineffective. The litany of inadequacies documented in the
pages that follow indicates that the chief asset of Canada's armed
forces is the stubborn loyalty of its men and women – a loyalty
which has little connection with their effectiveness. The dedication
of most of our service personnel is beyond question: their equipment is beyond salvage. Our forces have no mobilization plan,
cannot effectively intercept unannounced aircraft flying over our
territory, and are unable to enforce the 200-mile fishing limit at sea
or suppress acts of terror on land.

The popular notion that this country is far too large to be defended and, by some inexorable logic, is therefore safe from attack
does not hold up. "It's understandable why Canadians hesitate to
put their defence forces into anything like readiness," newspaper
columnist Douglas Fisher has commented. "We can't conceive of

it being necessary, and it undoubtedly isn't, insofar as we alone are concerned. But we're in a world where others are not forced to be so modest, and so collectively we have become the Ethelred the Unready of the well-to-do nations."

For most of the past thirty years, Canada has luxuriated in the comfortable notion that our military protection was the equivalent of joining a club: we are founding members of NATO, have more or less paid our dues, and are therefore immune from attack or criticism. The North Atlantic Alliance has hardly lived up to the ideals that brought it into being during the hopeful springtime of 1949, but, like democracy itself, the sixteen-nation "club" seems preferable to any of its alternatives. Still, it's worth asking whether or not any alternatives exist. Could we, for example, adopt the Swiss, Swedish, or Austrian solutions and become neutral? Could we follow the French option and remove ourselves from the Alliance, undertaking our own defence?

Neutrality is a seductively attractive idea: how splendid it would be to bid a permanent goodbye to all the rhetoric that pervades the aligned majority. Unfortunately, it isn't that simple. We are, yet again, the prisoners of our geography. Canada's territory provides for the United States the strategically essential "depth" granted to the USSR by its own Arctic. If we barred Americans from access to Canadian airspace for the early detection of hostile Soviet intentions, we would leave Washington little choice but to invade our territory. Short of such intrusion, the Soviets would hardly take our "neutrality" seriously. Unhappily, neutrality is a hollow option for Canada. It would be unacceptable to the United States and irrelevant to the Union of Soviet Socialist Republics.

These considerations aside, neutrality is an awesomely expensive choice. Europe's neutral countries spend at least twice as much per capita as NATO's partners do on defence. Austria, with a population of only 7.5 million, for example, maintains an armed force which at full mobilization strength would total 960,000. Fully 10.2% of Switzerland's population is permanently on military standby. Sweden and Switzerland have universal male conscription.

Another impractical alternative is the French solution. Under this we would be forced into having our own nuclear missiles and bearing heavier defence burdens than we would if we remained part of NATO – and we wouldn't have any of the compensating advantages.

It is a perversity of the current situation that what we gain in security as a nation from our current collective defence arrangements is considerably more than what we contribute.

As long as the principal threat we face is a nuclear attack on North America, our geography and our history dictate that, like it or not, we must rely for our security on the retaliatory capabilities of the United States and their underlying will to defend us. This is even more true if the threat is simply of a conventional war. That's why our membership in NATO is so essential. It is only our allegiance to this wider partnership that keeps us from being entirely under the American thumb. For the foreseeable future at least, the North Atlantic Alliance will remain the vital hinge of our defence arrangements.

Peace is a fragile commodity. Since the Second World War, 150 conventional conflicts have been fought, leaving twenty-five million dead. The longest uninterrupted period of peace since 1945 lasted scarcely twenty-six blessed days. According to the authoritative study on *World Military and Social Expenditures* carried out by Ruth Leger Sivard, an independent Washington commentator, there are now more than a hundred million men and women permanently engaged in military activities around the world. She calculates that since 1960, more than ten million people have died during sixty-five wars in forty-nine countries and that the international arms business currently accounts for an annual trade worth $150 billion. If re-armament continues at the current pace, national governments will have spent an additional $15 trillion for military preparedness by the end of this century.

During 1982, military expenditures totalled more than $500 billion; $1.5 billion per day or a million dollars per minute. To put this amount of money into more topical perspective: medical researchers have estimated that the eradication of smallpox cost the equivalent of only five hours of the arms race. Providing less-developed countries with fresh water and sanitation – the lack of which account for eighty per cent of all sickness in the world – would take three weeks of military expenditures.

Given these calculations, it is difficult not to shudder at the waste of potential benefits. It is also difficult not to feel that the probability of some kind of confrontation is preordained. War seems almost inevitable. The pace of military preparations is accelerating and taking dangerous new directions. A mind-boggling fifty thousand nuclear weapons are waiting to be used. By 1985, at least another two dozen countries will have gained the ability to manufacture and deliver them. To pretend that the Cold War's chief protagonists have grown so decisively powerful and the consequences of a nuclear exchange so grotesque that neither side would risk a shootout is the most vapid kind of wishful reasoning.

Defence strategy implies finding ways to avoid conflict. The doctrine of deterrence begins with the determination not to let the shooting start. Application of this doctrine has maintained an uneasy equilibrium for most of the past three decades, and it is only recently that the theory behind the doctrine has been called into question. Yet deterrence's validity hinges on both sides implicitly believing in it. The notion of deterrence is loosely based on an extension of the principle behind the maintenance of a strong internal police force: the most effective way of preserving "law and order" is to make the consequences of the use of force prohibitive. "Deterrence" may not be the most appealing of dogmas, but it works. For nearly thirty years now, the superpowers have kept one another at bay because to start shooting would bring unacceptable retribution. Canada's defence policy must fit into the philosophy of deterrence.

The urgency of the situation springs from the fact that, for the first time since the western alliance was forged in the spring of 1949, deterrence doesn't seem to work any more. NATO has decisively lost its military superiority over the Soviet empire. The professional bravado of the generals, admirals, and ambassadors who run NATO's bureaucratic headquarters in Brussels is increasingly affected by a confluence of military, political, and economic trends, which will culminate in what Henry Kissinger calls Russia's "window of opportunity." According to this theory, in 1984-85 Russia's military might will be at a peak and domestic economic problems will not yet have begun to constrain Soviet options. This

18

will be the ideal time-period for the USSR to go on the offensive.

Increasingly nervous about the credibility of the once-sacrosanct notion of mutual deterrence, political and military men both in the United States and in the USSR are swinging toward the terrifying dictum that the only truly believable deterrent to nuclear war is the willingness to fight one. We are facing a chess board on which every gambit is covered; no one feels free to make the first move.

The essence of our dilemma was caught in the autumn of 1982 in a comment by O. A. Hopkins, the protestant chaplain of Canada's armed forces. He was asked how, as a man of the cloth, he could have given his blessing to the first of the CF-18 jet interceptors to arrive in Ottawa. "There is little use in passing resolutions on vegetarianism," he replied, "when the wolves are of another opinion."

THE MILITARY IS Canada's largest organization. Its eighty thousand regulars (down from 126,000 in 1962) are spread among seventy stations and bases in Canada and Western Europe. (One thousand of these troops are involved in peace-keeping operations.) The defence department owns or leases 4.7 million acres of land; the replacement value of its non-military equipment is estimated at $6 billion.

As "Buzz" Nixon, a former Deputy Minister of National Defence, has pointed out: "The central problem of Canada's defence situation over the past fifteen, if not twenty, years is that budgets have been inadequate to maintain the size of Canadian Forces which would be required to give substantive effect to [the country's] declared policy. This inadequacy has occurred because defence and security have not been perceived by Canadians (both the people and the government) as issues which warrant being high on the list of national priorities. Defence has not been for some years a leading portfolio in Canada, as it is in most if not all NATO countries."

The politics of Canadian defence is disgraceful enough, but much of our military hardware is a bad joke. "We attack at dawn," runs the sarcastic toast in Canadian officers' messes these days. "That way, if things don't work out, we won't have wasted the whole day."

It is an appropriate sentiment:

- An American version of Canada's CF-104, which for another two years (until the new CF-18s come fully into service) will be our main air weapon in NATO, is considered so outdated that it has recently been added to the historical exhibits of the United States Air Force Museum in Dayton, Ohio.*
- The computers that operate the firing systems on most of our warships depend on antiquated vacuum tubes. Only two factories still turn out such obsolete equipment: one is located in Poland, the other in the USSR.
- Despite our climate and geography, our army has no oversnow vehicles. In one winter exercise, held on Melville Island in the Arctic, Canada's armoured personnel carriers managed to move less than thirty-five kilometres a day – about half the distance covered by a not particularly perky dogsled team.
- If we met our existing NATO commitments, fewer than three thousand troops would remain on Canadian soil to defend Canada's home territory in any future war. (It took sixteen thousand service personnel to provide security during the 1976 Summer Olympics in Montreal.)
- Although the Soviets have close to half a million undersea mines, at the moment our only defence against these deadly weapons is one squad of very nervous frogmen, groping around harbour bottoms with hand-held sonar sets.

There is a natural temptation to suppose that none of this is an immediate concern, that we will somehow scramble to readiness, if and when the need actually arises. It won't wash. Long gone are the days of 1914 and 1939, when eager Johnny Canucks and Rosie the Rivetters could slap together an instant military machine. If we don't have what we need on the day of an emergency, we're not going to have time to get it.

Defending Canada means not only repelling potential trans-

*We are not the only holdouts. Equivalents of the CF-104 also remain part of the Italian, Turkish, and West German forces.

gressors. It implies our willingness and our ability to stand our ground, to put a stamp of ownership on our own territory: to declare and protect Canadian sovereignty.

As François Mitterand, the President of France, said at the Hamburg Chamber of Commerce recently: "One must remember that at the end of the day, at the time of a decisive choice, a great country always finds itself alone – facing itself. . . ."

CHAPTER TWO

The Peaceable Kingdom

"Canada is an unmilitary community. Warlike her people have often been forced to be, military they have never been."
C.P. STACEY

T HE NOTION OF CANADA as a "peaceable kingdom" originated in the writings of Northrop Frye, the greatest of Canada's literary critics. He described an early nineteenth-century painting of that title by Edward Hicks which depicted Indians, Quakers, and animals – lions, bears, oxen, lambs, dogs – all reconciled with one another and the forces of nature. Frye saw in that painting a "haunting vision of serenity" which can also be seen as a recurring theme in Canadian literature.

Throughout Canada's history, we have pursued this quest for a peaceable kingdom. "Canada is an ummilitary community," wrote C.P. Stacey, Canada's pre-eminent military historian, at the beginning of the *Official History of the Canadian Army in the Second World War.* "Warlike her people have often been forced to be, military they have never been." We fought no war of independence, and our home-grown rebellions in Lower and Upper Canada before Confederation hardly qualify as major military actions. We have gone to war as a nation only when allies on other continents were threatened.

After Confederation, the first internal disturbances regarded by the central government as "threats to the state" were Riel's Red River Rebellion of 1870 and the Northwest Rebellion of 1884. The latter was important in the context of Prairie settlement and racial tensions of the time, but to call a three-day action at Batoche between adversaries each less than a thousand strong, a "battle," and to label the ten-day containment of a few score of police and civilians in the stockade at Battleford as a "siege," is pure over-dramatization. Other disturbances – the Quebec Conscription Riots of 1917, the Winnipeg General Strike of 1919, and the unemployment marches of the 1930s – may have terrified the governments of the time and indicated political or social crises, but they hardly constituted major military engagements in the history of nations. The most recent threat, the October Crisis of 1970, caused the government to invoke the War Measures Act in response to an "apprehended insurrection." Seven battalions of regular infantry were mobilized against a group of alleged insurrectionists numbering, according to military analyst John Gellner, "no more than three dozen."

Even though we have taken a voluntary hand in defending ourselves ever since 1651, when Pierre Boucher of Trois Rivières formed the beleaguered settlers into our first militia unit, the military mentality has never exercised an important influence in Canadian society. Nonetheless, our military record in overseas wars is second to none in valour and national effort. Between 1914 and 1918, the Canadian army demonstrated courage and sacrifice far beyond the call of duty. At Vimy Ridge, Ypres, Courcelette, Hill 70, the Somme, Passchendaele, and dozens of other battlefields, Canadians endured the hell of trench warfare, suffering an eventual 59,544 casualties. Some 172,950, mostly men, some women, came home wounded, many doomed to spend the rest of their lives in the dreary corridors of veterans' hospitals. Although it received little notice, a fledgling Canadian navy of 9,600 men fought that war too, many of its volunteers serving with the Royal Navy. Uniforms, discipline, and traditions were adopted from Britain's senior service without question or modification, setting the atmosphere of Canada's naval service for generations to come.

Despite Canada's considerable pre-war contribution to the pioneering of flight, no Canadian air force was established, but by the end of 1918, nearly twenty-three thousand Canadians had joined Britain's Royal Flying Corps. Ten of the Royal Air Force's twenty-seven official "aces," including Billy Bishop and Raymond Collishaw, were Canadians, each being credited with thirty or more "kills." After the war, when Canada decided to establish its own air force, it, too, was to be based on the British model, but, in contrast to the navy or the army, Canada didn't simply adopt the ways of the RAF. Since twenty-five per cent of the officers of the original Royal Flying Corps had been Canadian, they had had a good share in creating the joint traditions.

Between the two world wars the Canadian navy, militia, and air force barely managed to survive, but the scale of the Canadian war effort between 1939 and 1945 was awesomely impressive. Canada entered the war two years before the United States. From a population of ten million, more than one million men and women enlisted in our services, an overwhelming number of them volunteers. During the war, forty-two thousand died or were listed as missing. The Royal Canadian Navy, by 1945, was responsible for escorting four-fifths of the Atlantic convoys with a fleet of nearly a thousand destroyers, frigates, corvettes, and miscellaneous craft. The Royal Canadian Air Force contributed forty-five squadrons overseas. The British Commonwealth Air Training Plan produced 131,000 graduates, of whom more than half were Canadian. It was Canada's army that spearheaded the Dieppe raid and fought valiantly during the invasions of Sicily, Italy, and Normandy.

Despite the country's brave record (and eighty-six Victoria Crosses) in both world wars, there has never existed – except perhaps in the private musings of the few staff officers who have bothered to tackle the subject in unpublished essays – any perceived or proclaimed indigenous Canadian military strategy. The country's senior military training establishment, Royal Military College in Kingston, is now 110 years old, and has in the past produced many distinguished graduates in both the military and civilian worlds, but even so, Canadians have found themselves with no lasting heritage in the crafts of war – or even much of an instinct for self-defence. Canadian Legion parades these days draw more marchers than spectators.

The absence of any deep-rooted military tradition in this country is probably the single most important factor preventing any collective push for higher spending on national defence. There is also an absence of respect and interest towards the military on the part of both the public and many of our political leaders, from the top down. During the 1983 provincial election in British Columbia, New Democratic Party Leader David Barrett managed to generate laughs by quipping that "any country that buys submarines that leak and CF-18 airplanes that don't fly can't be all bad." The witticism accurately caught the stereotype of the armed forces in the minds of most Canadians. We tend to think of our military men and women – if we think of them at all – as short-haired amateurs, misfits who couldn't quite make it in civilian life, but who aren't basically warlike or particularly plausible about their profession. Hal Lawrence, one of Canada's Second World War heroes (he was awarded a Distinguished Service Cross for his part in the sinking of the U-94), once summed up this attitude in a letter to me:

> After Admiral H. T. W. Grant had retired as Chief of Naval Staff I was at his home one evening and asked him: "Why is it, sir, that when I'm in the UK and someone asks me what I do and I say I am a Lieutenant in the Royal Canadian Navy, he says, 'Oh, really, jolly good. You must come down for a weekend.' And when I'm asked the same question in the US and give the same reply, I'm told, 'Oh, good, you must come out and meet the little woman.'
>
> "But when the same question and answer are exchanged in Canada, there's an awkward pause while everyone thinks: 'Poor fellow. Probably didn't do well in Grade 12.'"
>
> "My dear Lawrence," the Admiral replied, "it has always been thus. In the UK, everyone knows the Navy and that it has kept them free for centuries; it doesn't matter if it's true or not. In the US, the military threw off the oppression of a distant tyrant and sailors have kept the tyrant out ever since. Again, it's not as simple as that, but that's what everyone believes. In Canada, on the other hand, we have always fought distant wars: in Egypt in the last century, in South Africa at the turn of the century, in Europe in 1914-18, in Europe, North Africa, and the Far East in 1939-45."
>
> "But what about the attack on Quebec by the Americans? What about the land and sea battles of 1812-14? What about our ships being sunk close to Quebec in 1939-45?"

"Few people know about that and fewer care. Have another glass of port and calm down."

THE MILITARY IN THIS COUNTRY operate outside the mainstream of society. Writing in the *Canadian Defence Quarterly*, two officers, Major-General Loomis and Lieutenant-Colonel Lightburn, recently took this argument in another direction, observing that military society in Canada has been set apart by its resemblance to a "secular religion." They stated that "an attempt has been made to integrate our military sub-culture into the main body of Canadian society: the sharp-toothed guard dog has been taken into the home to be made a family pet." This is a dubious proposition, since family pets, no matter how toothless, enjoy a playful fondness hardly accorded this country's armed forces, which have seldom attracted any public sentiment kinder than benign neglect. This has been true even at the highest level of Canadian politics. In his book, *Ministers and Generals*, Professor Desmond Morton documents at least two instances in earlier years when Canadian prime ministers have voiced the thoughts that Canada had no real need for defence forces of its own and that defence expenditures were really just another tool of the political reward system.

The use of our armed forces to support political, external, and industrial policies without the actual military requirements first being taken into account has been standard practice throughout Canadian history. Our political leaders have demonstrated an astonishing lack of confidence in their own military advisors. Writing about the War Committee of his own Cabinet at the height of the 1939-45 conflict, Prime Minister Mackenzie King confided to his diary: "I ruled out having the Canadian Chief of Staff present. It had been Heeney [then civilian secretary to the Cabinet] who had arranged for these meetings himself, as he said, just to give the Chiefs of Staff a 'look in' and let them feel important. The proceedings made it apparent that they were not needed and, by their not being present, the discussions were shortened."

It was not *because of* the country's political leadership, but *despite* it, that Canadians achieved such enviable reputations in two world wars.

In fact, our political history seems to indicate that we have a positive reluctance to choose a prime minister with any military associations. None of Canada's sixteen prime ministers have had significant senior military experience. (Curiously, the one with the most wartime service was Nobel Peace Prize winner Lester Pearson, who served for a time in the First World War as a junior officer, and who also had the closest personal associations with senior military officers.)

Canadians do not have the tradition of universal or compulsory military service that has been the experience of citizens of the United States, the United Kingdom, or for that matter, the Soviet Republics. For inescapable political reasons ours is an all-volunteer system, and even at the height of wartime emergencies, it has proved to be virtually impossible to introduce conscription.

During both world wars there was some resistance to compulsory military service in rural areas and in the labour movement throughout Canada, but the real opposition came from Quebec. Despite the distinguished military record of many French Canadians, Quebec has always been politically firm on this issue. During the First World War the Borden government, desperate for troop reinforcements for the trenches, initiated a move for conscription. The result was riots in Montreal and an absolute political rift between Quebec and the rest of Canada. Again, in the latter years of the Second World War, Mackenzie King, with his notorious phrase "conscription if necessary, but not necessarily conscription," attempted to provide conscripted support for overseas forces. Once again that implacable opposition to conscription occurred in Quebec. Quebec's recent history of enthusiastic support for René Lévesque, if not for all of his policies, suggests that there would be an equally strong refusal today to compulsory service in Canada's armed forces, regardless of the threat to national security.

THE LACK OF RELEVANCE under which our professional military must operate flows from one of Canadian society's deepest-rooted convictions: that we are a cultural free port, a society so open that our citizens need claim no loyalties, not even a belief in their own country. In his introduction to *Canada: A Landscape Portrait*, Robert Fulford, the editor of *Saturday Night*, spotlighted this attitude by describing the differences noted by American draft dodgers who came here during the Vietnam War.

What they noticed first about Canada was the absence of a compulsion to conform. They discovered to their surprise that patriotism is not a prerequisite of Canadian citizenship. What the draft dodgers found in Canada was a unique kind of psychic freedom, a rather different matter from political freedom. It is this freedom, expressed in ethnic, linguistic, and regional terms, that forms the real basis of Canadian life.

The curious fact is that, in order to qualify as Canadians, we are not required to be loyal, even in theory, to the idea of Canada. At an editorial meeting at *Maclean's* early in the 1960s, the then-new subject of Quebec separatism was introduced. One editor declared firmly that separatists should be prosecuted for treason. He was an English immigrant, still innocent in Canadian ways, and his suggestion was greeted with derisive laughter, but it occurred to me at the time that if one looked at his views from a global perspective they were not altogether preposterous. In a very few countries would the idea of national dismemberment be greeted with such insouciance. But in fact, by unspoken agreement, Canadian citizenship carries the ultimate freedom: the freedom to declare that one doesn't want to be Canadian, to urge that one's region should cease to be part of Canada, and yet to go on being a Canadian and receiving the appropriate benefits.

This notion – that "patriotism is not a prerequisite of Canadian citizenship" – is one of the fundamental differences between Americans and Canadians. It pervades everything that we are, do, and hope to become.

THE EVOLUTION OF THE CONTRASTING ATTITUDE in the United States is relevant to our current impasse. The most violent clash of arms during the nineteenth century was the American Civil War. As well as those four years of bloody internal combat, during the

29

two centuries since the United States won independence, its regulars have gone to war in sixty-nine Indian campaigns and seven foreign wars – Tripoli, Mexico, Spanish-America, First and Second World Wars, Korea, and Vietnam. Ten American presidents (including the country's founder) were military men. Two other military men, Admiral Dewey and General MacArthur, actively sought its highest office. "That we are a violent people," American historian Barbara Tuchman has written,

> is undeniable, and the reason for this goes back to the beginning. The first settlers of the American wilderness bore arms on their own behalf. Every man owned a gun to defend his home and family against Indian attack as well as to provide game for food; each community appointed a captain for common defence. Military action was personal and vital, not imposed in drilled ranks and chalked white pantaloons for some remote dynastic or territorial ambition of a monarch. Conquest of the plains took fifty years of incessant warfare. Eventually, when the Civil War released armed men to the frontier, the struggle was won by the fort, the repeating rifle, starvation, treachery, the railroad, the reservation policy and, ultimately, the extermination of the buffalo which had provided the Plains Indian with food, shelter, and clothing. The last battle was fought in 1890 – less than one hundred years ago.

This was not the Canadian experience; the settlement of the Canadian West (and North) followed a quite different pattern. As social historian William Kilbourn has pointed out: "A visitor to pioneer Saskatchewan remarked at the strange sight of a sod hut with a big Canadian Bank of Commerce sign on it, open for business. The essence of the Canadian West is in that image. Organized society usually arrived with the settlers or ahead of them – not only the branch bank manager, but the mounted policeman and the railway agent, the priest, and the Hudson's Bay factor."

Quite apart from this essential difference in the genesis of the two countries, the United States went on to express – and occasionally implement – its territorial ambitions, while Canada was never tempted to stake any external claims of its own. The Monroe Doctrine and the teachings on the importance of naval power of Admiral Alfred Thayer Mahan captured the imagination of Americans as they annexed Hawaii, Panama, Cuba, Puerto Rico, the Philippines, and even won the right (after the Boxer Rebellion of 1900) to maintain a regiment in mainland China.

None of this should imply either that American military men are gun-happy, macho, fighting machines, or that Canadians have a benign and innocent view of the world. Canada may not have had any imperial or territorial ambitions, but Canadians shared in British imperial ambitions and adventures: we sent voyageurs up the Nile in an attempt to rescue General Gordon, and Canadian troops went to South Africa to support the British cause in the Boer War. Our swift entry into the First and Second World Wars in Europe was the result of our rôle in the British Empire, not because of any serious threat to our own territory.

THE REASON FOR THE ABSENCE of any clear approach to the defence of our own country is based on the fortunate fact that our temperament and geography have interacted to confer on Canada, throughout most of its history, relative immunity from invasion. Before the advent of the very long-range bomber and the intercontinental ballistic missile, Canadians were seldom, even in the darkest days of two world wars, seriously worried about the prospect of direct military attack. At the same time, our historical experience has been that of a state which has rarely felt the need to rely solely or even primarily on its own resources for its security. Defence was either an Imperial concern, which meant mainly the responsibility of Britain, or was assured, at least implicitly, by the Monroe Doctrine of the United States. The rapid escalation of Soviet military capabilities following the onset of the Cold War in the late 1940s hardly altered Canada's attitude to defence. Certainly, it was recognized that the immunity from air attack Canada had enjoyed for so many generations had come to an end, but as long as the USSR's might was limited to long-range bombers, it seemed like an answerable threat. A series of bilateral pacts were negotiated, leading to the 1951 agreement to establish the Pinetree Radar Line and culminating in the NORAD agreement of 1957, which brought Canada and the United States into an integrated air defence system. During this period, Canada's defence expenditures were proportionately much greater than at present, reaching 7.6 per cent of the GNP ($1,907 million) in 1953 during the Korean War. In the postwar period we still felt that our military rôle should be an active one relating to our allies and, despite the obsession with potential atomic attacks, we believed in the power of conventional forces in conjunction with anti-bomber defence systems, and had no hesitation in sending our troops overseas to maintain our commitments. But by the late 1950s, the early intercontinental ballistic missiles had appeared on the scene. The Soviets had launched Sputnik, demonstrating that ICBM technology was within their grasp. The so-called missile gap between the USSR and the USA was perceived and the first questions about the ultimate value of anti-bomber defences in a missile age were beginning to be heard.

It was the Cuban missile crisis of 1962 that marked the turning point in the relationship between the world's superpowers. This dramatic standoff led to the present condition of relatively stable mutual deterrence between the Soviet Union and the United States. The by-product for this country was the notion, now solidly entrenched within the Canadian mentality, that no matter what Canada did, our fate would be determined by the actions of the United States. This resulted in a tendency to view Canada's contributions to collective defence, whether in North America or in NATO, as being either of marginal importance or dispensable altogether. Most of Canada's politicians began to look upon the armed forces as an encumbrance which had to be lugged along in pursuit of various foreign-policy goals, but which was to be kept as light as possible. As Professor James Eayrs so aptly summed it up, "the major function of the Canadian military establishment has had practically nothing to do with our national security and practically everything to do with supporting and sustaining our national diplomacy."

With political priorities other than national security occupying the forefront of their concerns, Canadian political leaders were able to reduce defence to a back-burner priority. They traded on the strategic advantage which, alone among the allies of the United States Canada possesses – geographic propinquity. John Anderson, an Assistant Deputy Minister of Defence, once summed it up this way:

> Accidents of geography and history have placed Canada, in strategic terms, next to one of the two most powerful military nations of the world – as well as between it and the other most powerful military nation across the most probable routes of direct military attack by one upon the other. The principal, if not the only, direct military threat to Canada's national security is that incidental to a nuclear war between these two super-powers and, more particularly, to a strategic nuclear attack by the Soviet Union against the United States. Canada, at one and the same time, is unable either to escape the consequences of such an attack, or by its own efforts to prevent such an attack from occurring. Thus, to a degree greater than perhaps any other state, Canada is incapable of establishing its security requirements in terms of a direct defence of its national territory against the known military capabilities of a potential enemy. The consequence is that there is really no way for the Canadian defence analyst to define objectively either an upper or a lower limit to the amount of resources which Canada should expend on its own defence.

Sensible as that analysis may be, it has become the rationale for depriving us of any clear-cut security imperatives of our own. Getting their political bosses to assign any value to Canada's military contributions is the on-going dilemma facing the country's few serious defence planners. The issue of how relevant to the protection of Canada our military expenditures really are, and the question of how marginal our utility in the West's overall defence posture has become – these are the arguments under constant discussion at National Defence Headquarters in Ottawa.

The Peaceable Kingdom cannot be achieved through apathy or by default. Like any realm, imaginative or political, its existence must be the result of effort, deliberation, and policy.

CHAPTER THREE

Bucks for Bangs

The existing defence budget, at $8 billion, happens to coincide precisely with the estimate by the RCMP of the amount of illegal street drugs sold in Canada during 1982.

CANADA'S DEFENCE EXPENDITURES in 1983 will total about $8 billion, which at 1.8% of gross national product ranks us as the lowest among NATO allies. Budget increases call for a $10-billion outlay by 1985, but there will be no proportionate improvement.

Compared with much smaller and poorer NATO countries, the level of our military expenditures takes on a decidedly shabby dimension. Of our total population of 25 million, we have 80,000 personnel in our regular armed forces and roughly 19,000 in the reserves. In contrast, Denmark, with a population of 5 million, fields an armed force of 35,100 with 154,500 reserves; Norway has a population of 4 million, a regular force of 37,000, and 247,000 reserves; the Netherlands, with a population of 14 million, has a regular force of 103,000, with 171,000 in reserves; Belgium, with a population of 10 million, boasts a force of 87,900 with 115,500 in reserves. Considering the percentages of populations between the ages of 18 and 45, 1.5% of Canada's eligible manpower is in its armed forces; 3.3% of Denmark's; 5% of Norway's; 3.8% of the Netherlands; and 4.5% of Belgium's.

Peacetime budgets in Canada have not always been so limited. Defence expenditures as a share of the federal budget reached a peacetime high of forty-three per cent in 1953. In 1961, Canada's armed forces had a permanent strength of approximately 126,000, with defence expenditures accounting for twenty-seven per cent of the federal budget. By 1963, these costs started dropping but they still accounted for twenty-one per cent of budgetary items. The

Royal Canadian Navy, for example, consisted of an aircraft carrier, forty-three anti-submarine escorts, ten minesweepers (with another ten on order), as well as many smaller craft. Defence was operating under an authorized budget of 124,000 person-years, as opposed to less than 80,000 person-years twenty years later. Under Paul Hellyer's devastating stewardship, the reserves were cut from 60,000 to 20,000 personnel.

The department began to encounter severe budgetary problems in the mid-sixties. Total defence spending had declined steadily from the Korean War peak, while personnel and operating expenses continued to consume an ever-increasing proportion of the budget. At the same time, with diminishing resources for capital spending, the department found it very difficult to replace worn-out and obsolete equipment. Given these adverse trends and wanting to restore a better balance between personnel and equipment spending, in 1964 Hellyer announced the first "formula funding plan."

Under this five-year program, overall defence spending was to increase by 2% a year from a starting figure of $1,550 million. Hellyer's goal was to raise equipment spending to one-quarter of the total defence budget by way of the 2% annual growth figure and the savings generated by unification. These capital funds would, in theory, have enabled the government to undertake a five-year, $1.5-billion equipment procurement plan. This capital target was not even remotely approached – indeed, the capital portion of the defence budget actually decreased from 19.9% to 14.2% between 1965 and 1970 – so that to stay below their overall budgetary ceiling, the regular forces had to decrease manpower levels by 20,000.

By 1969, soaring social security costs prompted the new Trudeau administration to consider a firmer stance on overall government spending. As part of this program of fiscal restraint, the defence budget was to be "frozen" for three years at $1,815 million a year. This level, while somewhat (8.2%) above the 1969 budget, included no provisions for price or cost increases. Although the ceiling was actually exceeded by $200 million over the three-year period, manpower levels were reduced by 10,641. Hardest hit was the capital component, which fell from $253.3 million in 1970 to

$151.4 million in 1973 (or 7.6% of the total defence budget), the lowest level since the Korean War.

By the fall of 1973, it was becoming increasingly clear that, contrary to the hopes in the 1971 White Paper, "multiple-tasking" would not compensate the Canadian Forces for their severe equipment deficiencies. Recognizing that the credibility of the forces was in jeopardy, Defence Minister James Richardson announced a "modernization and renewal program." Under it, the total defence budget was to increase by seven per cent annually.

The novel element of this formula related to the differential escalation rates allocated to the main budgetary categories, with personnel costs allowed to increase by six per cent a year and the operations and maintenance category by four per cent, with the balance allocated to the capital category. By assigning the bulk of the overall seven per cent annual increase to long-overdue equipment purchases – it was estimated that the formula would increase capital expenditures by roughly seventeen per cent each year (twelve per cent for real growth and five per cent for inflation) – the government hoped capital spending would nearly double to twenty per cent of the defence budget by the end of the five-year period.

Within a few months of launching this new formula, it proved inadequate for keeping pace with the enormous inflationary shock which hit the Canadian economy in 1974. Despite additional manpower cutbacks, a drastic thirty-per-cent curtailment of operational activities and training, and some further reduction and stretching out of equipment procurement programs, the defence department still required a sizeable supplementary appropriation ($375 million) to ride out the inflationary storm.

By the fall of 1975, it became obvious that Ottawa's existing financing arrangements could not generate the funds required for the many major equipment replacement projects considered essential for maintaining the operational effectiveness of the forces – could not even meet inflation's effects. Under a new interim funding formula, the personnel, operations, and maintenance portion of the defence budget was to be increased annually by just enough to compensate for inflation, while the capital portion would be increased by twelve per cent in real terms for a five-year period.

The short-lived Conservative government, elected in 1979, terminated the interim funding formula and, in its place, brought in a new "Expenditure Management System." It was to have its own annually updated, four-year "resource envelope" for expenditure planning. Upon their return to power in 1980, the Liberals retained this idea, pledging that the defence budget would grow by three per cent in real terms each year.

This modest total has not been achieved and the equipment budget remains grossly inadequate.

The existing defence budget, at $8 billion, happens to coincide precisely with estimates by the RCMP of the amount of illegal street drugs sold in Canada during 1982. That Canadians should spend as much for pot and other mind-blowers as for defence is as handy an indicator as any of how urgently our priorities need to be rearranged.

CHAPTER FOUR

The Boys in Green

It is the supreme irony of the Canadian defence situation that, literally, the only clear-cut political decision on defence policy any government has made in the past twenty years was on unification of the armed forces – and it has been a disaster.

W HAT ARE THE CONSEQUENCES to our military personnel of being given so little priority by government, and so little attention by the Canadian public? (Challenge any well-informed Canadian to name any one of our last six chiefs of defence staff.) John Shepherd, chairman of the board of Leigh Instruments Ltd. and a director of the Canadian Institute for Economic Policy, has pointed out:

The Canadian military is largely divorced from Canadian society. It has no strength in the Cabinet and no political following. It does not appear to be relevant to the key issues and priorities of the day. It is not focussed as a significant national factor and is rigidly committed to current strategies.

This is an inevitable result of the isolation of our generals and admirals. Even the most intelligent among these senior officers are defiant in their conviction that their main problem is public misunderstanding and apathy. They stick to their own. Caught up by the private jokes, inside gossip, and little niceties that make up peacetime life in the forces, they are committed by an unwritten code to a way of life outside the Canadian mainstream. They study thick volumes of intelligence reports and seem to understand every country but their own.

The ultimate expression of the Canadian military mind is the

National Defence Headquarters building in Ottawa.* The downtown skyscraper is a strange place, even when considered among the array of the capital's bureaucratic fortresses. The structure is an extraordinarily inefficient maze of cubbyholes – an airless, emotion-defying concrete block filled with paper kingdoms. Its occupants have acronyms instead of names and the building itself seems buffeted by moods instead of weather. The barometer is always falling. One is reminded of an observation by the philosopher Santayana: "The workings of the great institutions are mainly the result of a vast mass of routine, petty malice, self-interest, carelessness, and sheer mistakes. Only a residual fraction is thought."

There is nothing particularly threatening about the men and women who occupy defence headquarters – except perhaps, their level of frustration. The most conscientious of them feel torn apart by their sworn duty to defend the country they love, knowing that they are unable to do so with the facilities at hand. Others have given up and are merely putting in the time necessary to collect their pensions. The majority are doing their best under inordinately difficult circumstances. This attitude was most succinctly expressed by Lieutenant-General Charles Belzile, Chief of the Mobile Command, when he was testifying before a recent House of Commons Committee. Having been asked whether he would feel more secure commanding a much larger, more effective body of men, he replied: "There is no doubt that I would feel considerably better with larger forces. However, it is not my job to state so. It is a political decision, and my job, as humbly as I can state it, is to click my heels and do the best I can with what I have. This I can guarantee."

A good answer, but hardly a sentiment to warm the soul in these cold days of East-West confrontation. The trait which makes Canada unique in the context of the arms race is that, alone among the world's armed forces, ours are totally "unified." It is the supreme irony of the Canadian defence situation that, literally, the only

*The building was originally designed for the Ministry of Transport for its new head office. The defence department had several more appropriate designs of its own rejected.

clear-cut political decision on defence policy any government has made in the past twenty years was on unification of the armed forces – and it has been a disaster.

In March 1964, Paul Hellyer, then the Pearson government's Minister of National Defence, tabled a White Paper which outlined in precise detail his plan "to integrate the armed forces of Canada under a single chief of defence staff," as a first step "toward a single unified defence force."

Integration was not a bad idea. It meant doing away with the triplication of such support services as the medical corps, the chaplain service, supply, pay, and other staff functions that had existed separately for each of the army, the navy, and the air force, with an inevitably appalling overlap and wastage. Integration of these support services represented a significant improvement in the efficiency and modernization of Canada's armed forces. Legislation creating the integrated command structure was passed on July 16 of that year and Air Chief Marshal Frank Miller, previously chairman of the Chiefs of Staff Committee, became the first Chief of the Canadian Defence Staff. Hellyer was careful to point out that this meant "the three services [were] no longer independent entities for the purpose of control and administration."

The issue didn't become controversial until mid-1966, when the Conservative Opposition, which had a high proportion of veterans, finally grasped that Hellyer was really serious about doing away with individual services, establishing "one force with one common name, a common uniform, and common rank designations." The navy, army, and air force would henceforth be known as "the sea element," "the land element," and "the air element," and each "element" would be responsible for defending its "environment." Sailors who had proudly worn ships' names on their cap tallies for more than half a century would now wear the common peaked cap over common green uniforms; regiments with more than a century of tradition would be disbanded and redistributed. Rank nomenclature would lose its meaning by being reduced to a common denominator.

Rear-Admiral William Landymore, a distinguished naval officer who had been fired five years ahead of usual retirement age for opposing Hellyer, set out the most valid arguments against the unification scheme.

Within the services, the threat of this single force is devastating. The single force threatens the psychological basis of military life. The confusion and insecurity already caused among career-conscious officers and men is the immediate reason why so many more are leaving the service and not being replaced by recruits. The concept of the single force is based on a naïve and limited view of the armed services – not as forces to defend the nation in time of war, but primarily as a special peacetime force to undertake small police actions in foreign countries.

The frightening thing about this aspect of the single-force plan is that it assumes present conditions among the nations of the world will remain as they are. What happens when the status quo alters? And we can be sure that it will. Instead of the flexible military organizations we have at present, are we to be left with no more than a contingent of unemployed constables in green suits?

Seven admirals as well as half a dozen air marshals and generals joined Landymore in condemning Hellyer's unification scheme, and extensive hearings of the Commons Defence Committee were held to air their complaints. But Hellyer was unyielding. "The minister," wrote *Globe and Mail* columnist George Bain, "has got to the point of being tough merely for the sake of being tough – or perhaps for the sake of the image he hopes will propel him into the Liberal leadership: that of a strong, resolute, decisive man."

Landymore kept insisting that unification was inconsistent and impractical, and that the defence minister had not thought through its consequences. During their final meeting, Landymore asked Hellyer: "Give me one reason, one fact, one objective of yours – one way in which unification is going to make our armed forces more efficient and more economical."

"Just wait," Hellyer replied, "every country in the world will copy us."

We are still waiting.

Nearly two decades later, no other country has adopted the

unification idea and put on common uniforms. Any serious student of military psychology analyzing the elements that go into the making of an effective soldier, airman, or sailor has concluded that it is critically important to allow any combat unit to develop kinship and solidarity. That's why every other army, navy, and air force in the world makes it a point to foster stable social structures – regiments, ships' companies, and squadrons – each developing individual pride of service and collective esprit de corps.

Canada's navy was the hardest hit by unification because its basic morale unit has always been the service itself. Sailors in Halifax derisively refer to their green uniforms as "costumes" and cast envious glances at the blue dress of the Dartmouth ferryboat crews. In a 1982 survey of the West-Coast maritime facilities, an overwhelming ninety-six per cent of personnel of all ranks (half of whom had never worn anything but the dark green outfits) voted for a return to the traditional blues – even if they had to buy them with their own funds.

Captain Michael Hadley, a West-Coast historian who has commanded Canadian naval ships, told a recent parliamentary committee:

> I have just returned from Europe, where I spend some time associated with our NATO counterparts. I was struck by the fact that the navy is an international force – the navy in blue. But over the years the Canadian Navy has isolated itself symbolically by wearing green. When a man is isolated from his symbols, something happens to his psyche. A Navy like ours, which has lost its symbols, is symptomatic of a Navy which has lost its strength, its power, and its morale. The two are related. We have to return somehow to the situation where the Navy is brought back into its international community of sailors.

It's easy enough to dismiss complaints against the green uniforms as outdated nostalgia for Beau Geste traditions. But Winston Churchill was right when he said that an army is not like a limited liability company to be reconstructed, remodeled, liquidated, and inflated from week to week as money markets fluctuate – that it is not an inanimate thing like a house to be pulled down or enlarged or structurally altered at the caprice of its owner. "It is a living thing," he said. "If it is bullied, it sulks; if it is unhappy, it pines; if it is harried, it gets feverish; and if it is sufficiently disturbed, it will dwindle in strength."

There is a simple but significant social contract negotiated between a democracy and the person who decides to join its national military forces: a willingness to die for one's country. As Sir John Hackett, the British military futurist, has pointed out:

> Whatever the contract of the military professional says about terms of service, rights, duties, rewards, obligations, privileges, and so on, the military institution is dominated by an unwritten clause. This sets out an unlimited liability. It requires of a man that he be prepared to surrender life itself if the discharge of his duty should demand that. This is not often invoked in peacetime, but its existence lends a dignity to the military condition which is difficult to deny.

Men under fire don't risk their lives for their country – and they most certainly don't die for "environments." They fight for their buddies. They defend the psychological bonding that takes place between individuals caught up in common cause. The outward symbol of that cause is their uniform – a symbol of which Canadians have now been stripped.

CHAPTER FIVE

Naval Gazing

"If somebody gave me total power to go to Russia and destroy their armed forces, I'd order the Russian forces unified, put them into green uniforms, place them on a fixed budget, and leave."

REAR-ADMIRAL WILLIAM HUGHES

S MALLER THAN THE British Columbia ferry system, Canada's navy has been left behind by the advancing technology of war at sea. Of our twenty fighting ships, all but four are between nineteen and twenty-seven years old; their hulls have become so thin and shaky that masking tape has had to be used to keep seawater from damaging electronic instruments.

While these destroyers retain a fair anti-submarine capability, they have no defence at all against Exocet-style missiles and wouldn't last an hour in the kind of weapons exchange that took place in the Falklands War. (The first of the new generation of anti-missile missiles won't become part of the Canadian fleet until 1988.) Based on a 1953 design, most of the destroyers which, except for three semi-obsolete submarines, make up Canada's entire fighting fleet, were built between 1956 and 1964. The current "extended life" conversion program is a questionable manoeuvre. HMCS *Restigouche*, for example, commissioned in 1958 and originally due to be phased out in 1984, is now to remain in service until 1994 – thirty-six years at sea.

The Canadian ships are too old even for their skippers to judge which fatigue problems will develop next. NATO considers Canada's navy to be employing, in the jargon of the trade, vessels at their "end-of-life condition." Three of the destroyers counted as part of our NATO fleet are permanently docked so they can be cannibalized for parts to keep the other ships going a while longer.

45

Even the best of the destroyers have been experiencing thirty per cent "downtime" for dockside repairs. In the autumn of 1981 when sixteen destroyers had to stay in port with cracked boilers, the *Globe and Mail* wisecracked: "We can only hope that a potential enemy will be too overcome with merriment at Canada's predicament to get up to serious mischief. If on Christmas Day you saw three ships go sailing by, it might well have been three-quarters of our destroyer strength. At the moment, six out of the twenty are reported to be on active service, which ought to make Switzerland think twice about trying anything, but we are assured that many of the fourteen others would be able to leap out of dry dock at short notice to deal with an emergency. Canada's instant fleet – just add water."

Such send-ups are particularly galling when set against the Royal Canadian Navy's past achievements. Although a separate service was not established until 1910, the use of naval vessels in Canadian waters has a long history. A 500-ton corvette was launched in 1739 and several major fighting vessels were built in New France during the next few years, including the 700-ton *Caribou*. The outbreak of the American Revolution greatly stimulated inland shipbuilding and in 1814, the *St. Lawrence* was launched at Kingston as flagship of the British naval forces on the Great Lakes. She was a three-decker of 2,300 tons, mounting 102 guns – comparable to Lord Nelson's *Victory*. On the coasts, the Royal Navy, with bases at Halifax on the Atlantic and Esquimalt on the Pacific, provided naval defence. In 1909, Canada decided to establish her own navy and a year later the Naval Service Act passed, amidst vicious political infighting which contributed to the defeat of the Laurier government in 1911. The first Royal Canadian Navy consisted of the *Niobe* and the *Rainbow,* an obsolete Royal Navy light cruiser of the Apollo class, launched in 1891, which cost Canada only £50,000.

During the First World War, the young RCN played a limited role, mainly on anti-submarine patrol on the East Coast. Only one ship and 150 men were lost. In the years between the wars, the navy, like the other services, suffered from severe cutbacks. But, when the Liberal government undertook a re-armament program after 1936, the RCN was particularly favoured. By 1939, the RCN had six modern destroyers and four minesweepers. In the Second

World War, the RCN enlisted 106,522 men and by 1945 it was operating 428 ships – the world's third-largest navy.* Six destroyers were sent to Great Britain after the fall of France in June 1940. In the summer of 1941, the RCN organized the Newfoundland Escort Force for convoy duty. By 1942, Canada was doing forty per cent of the convoy work on the North Atlantic and by the end of the war nearly all of it. The RCN escorted 25,000 merchant ships carrying 200 million tons of supplies across the Atlantic; it sank twenty-seven submarines and forty-two Nazi surface ships. By 1945, the RCN had lost thirty-one ships and 2,025 men in action. The RCN did not disappear immediately after the Second World War. In the early fifties, defence minister Brook Claxton called for a hundred-ship navy, with fifty-two of them seconded to NATO. We didn't get them, and our naval force has been declining steadily over the past thirty years.

As Vice-Admiral James Andrew Fulton, one of the most capable and conscientious officers ever to head Canada's Maritime Command, commented upon retiring in July of 1983: "The Canadian navy has been reduced from 'state-of-the-art' to 'tail-end' status because of a lack of will on the part of the federal government and the lack of support of the Canadian people. We simply have not got the necessary equipment to keep up with the modern threat."

CANADA'S INTERNATIONAL TRADE now accounts for twenty-nine per cent of our gross national product, much of it moving by sea, including all of the oil imports to the Maritimes and nearly half of Quebec's petroleum products. Such ocean traffic would become essential in wartime. NATO's ability to sustain itself would depend on rushing troops and equipment across the Atlantic. Admiral J. C. Wood, when he was Chief, Maritime Doctrine and Operations, testified before a parliamentary committee that,

> it is planned to move the bulk of war equipment needed for reinforcement by sea in approximately 700 ships. As an exam-

---

*In total, we had 2 aircraft carriers, 2 cruisers, 3 armed merchant cruisers, 26 destroyers, 71 frigates, 122 corvettes, 85 minesweepers, 16 armed yachts, and about 100 motor torpedo boats.

ple, 1.4 million men would be required to be airlifted. Some 4.5 million tons of their initial supplies by sea and 4.5 million tons of ammunition must be moved by sea. Six hundred thousand barrels of fuel per day will have to be delivered to Europe to support them. To sustain reinforcement, approximately 4.2 million short tons of supplies will be required per month. Experts say 97% of re-supply tonnages must be sea-borne. This will involve approximately 350 ships in full-time service between North America and Europe.*

Ten years ago NATO could have attempted all its maritime tasks with a good expectation of success. That it cannot do so now is a measure of the growth of Soviet sea-denial (the jargon for military control of the sea) achievements. Canada's Maritime Command estimates that on any given day, 300 to 400 ships are inside our East-Coast territorial limits and that at least one-fifth of them are Russian. One NATO report has concluded that Soviet submarines are penetrating under the polar icecap as far south as Baffin Bay. No Canadian naval vessel has ice-breaking capability, leaving our vast northern waters without any surface surveillance.

In fact, our capacity for surveying, let alone defending, our territorial waters is hopeless. The two-hundred-mile limit embraces almost six million square miles of "territory," and our navy is not equipped to monitor even a fraction of that area.

Our gaps in maritime preparedness include the lack of a merchant fleet (only eight deep-sea ships are still sailing under a Canadian flag). Only four of the fisheries department's vessels are ocean-going. Our Coast Guard is woefully inadequate. Although we boast the world's second longest coastline, some of the worst sea conditions, and extensive inland waterways, the Coast Guard has only thirty-nine rescue ships; Holland maintains twenty-nine rescue vessels for an ocean coastline of just 240 miles.

The distribution of the meager maritime capabilities we do have is badly out of balance, between the East and West coasts. No

---

*To reduce some of this dependence on sea supplies, the United States has pre-positioned enough equipment on the European Central Front for four armoured divisions and is currently pre-positioning similar equipment for a full marine brigade in Norway.

submarines or ship-mounted helicopters are stationed on Vancouver Island, and only four of the eighteen Aurora naval patrol aircraft are kept on station there. The Commander, Maritime Forces Pacific, is responsible for the protection of shipping in an area of more than a million square miles of ocean over which travels thirty-one per cent of Canada's exports. Based on current shipping levels of coal, grains, sulphur, potash, phosphate, alumina, and crude oil, a minimum of seventeen hundred vessel-roundtrips annually now fall within this protection area. It is essential that our naval forces be much more evenly distributed between the East and the West coasts. At present, the emphasis is placed much too strongly on the Atlantic.

In the summer of 1983, mainly as a measure that would help revive Canada's dormant shipyards, the Trudeau government finally approved construction of six 4,200-ton patrol frigates that have been on the drawing boards since 1972. In 1977, when the program was first costed out, the total expenditure came to $1.58 billion. Now the ships are budgeted at $6 billion, and by the time the last hull is delivered in 1992, no doubt that cost will have doubled. By then, only four of the navy's existing destroyers will even be able to float. Canada would then have an effective fleet of ten ships, of which at least a third are traditionally in port for refitting. That would leave six ships divided among three coasts.

The tremendous technological advances which have so altered and increased the hazards of war at sea also make forward planning emphatically more challenging. The Senate Sub-Committee on National Defence, in a recent report, described some of the changes that have already taken place.

Canadians who think about their navy in the Second World War, tend to carry an image of the spume-swept bridge of a corvette (laid down six months before, built by a brewer, and paid for by nickles and pennies contributed by elementary students from rural Prince Edward Island), occupied by young bankers, school teachers, farm boys from the Prairies and a crusty old fisherman, none of whom (except for the crusty old fisherman) had ever seen the sea until joining the navy ninety days before. Binoculars clamped to their keen eyes, strong stomachs coping with the violent pitching of the tiny grey vessel, they sailed off to be hidden in the mists of the North Atlantic. Not all that far from the truth. At the outbreak of World War II, Canada's regular navy had 6 destroyers and 2,600 uniformed personnel. By 1945, there were 211 vessels of significant size in commission and more than 94,000 men and women in naval uniforms.

Such scenes, even making allowances for rose-coloured glasses, will not be seen again. The ship will have taken eight years to design, at least three to build, and will have cost as much as the annual budget of a good-sized Canadian city. Instead of the open bridge, there will be a compartment deep within the ship's gas-tight citadel, fed by recycled, filtered air. Instead of the binoculars, there will be cathode ray tubes displaying the computerized images provided by a half-dozen or more sensor systems. The men whose faces will be caught in the dull red light of the room and the flickering green of the display terminals will be professional military with years of experience and training in electronics, mathematics and physics, computer science, and engineering. The ship will not sail off into the mists to be lost from view. The mists will be penetrated by space satellites; the sounds of the ship will be heard by a submarine 160 km away; infra-red scanners of aircraft hours away from their home landing strip will seek it out. This ship and this team of men cannot be thrown together overnight. If they are, they will not likely sail back into harbour.

The six new patrol frigates are a welcome, if overdue, addition, but their configuration and armaments have been frozen in the present state-of-the-art: they must be built exactly the way they were designed. By the time the last of the bunch goes to sea – nine years from now – naval strategy will have moved so far into the future that we will have achieved the absurd: we will have launched a brand new fleet of already-obsolete ships.

Other countries, principally Britain, have bypassed the problem of what's referred to as "bloc obsolescence" by turning out at least one new ship a year. This way, no undigestible financial lump has to pass through the system all at one time. Since ships are retired at a relatively younger age, it gives the Royal Navy's reserve more up-to-date equipment on which to train. This is a system we desperately need.

In the United States, the defence build-up planned by President Reagan directs half its budget over the next five years towards ship construction. The intention is to float a mighty 600-ship fleet, organized around 15 carrier-centred task forces. That will require the acquisition of 210 new ships at an annual cost set somewhere between $12 and $23 billion. In addition to its regular patrol duties in the Indian, Pacific, North and South Atlantic Oceans, the Mediterranean Sea, and the Persian Gulf, the U.S. Navy is to be utilized as the prime method of enforcing America's forty-eight mutual defence pacts.

The ambitions of our own admirals are much less grandiose. They just want to stay afloat. "We're facing fifteen years of benign neglect," declared Rear-Admiral William Hughes, shortly before he was fired for saying so. "In those years there has been tremendous technological change and tremendous change in the operational capability of the potential opposition. If somebody gave me total power to go to Russia and destroy their armed forces, I'd order the Russian forces unified, put them into green uniforms, place them on a fixed budget, and leave."

CHAPTER SIX

The Army's Aches

The pledges we have made to NATO for troop reinforcements on its Central and Northern flanks would leave precisely two infantry battalions stationed in Canada – less than two thousand men charged with the land defence of half a continent.

NO REAL CANADIAN ARMY HAS EXISTED since unification, but for purposes of discussion the term is still useful. Of the nine different commands that now make up the Canadian Armed Forces, three are "environmental" (sea, air, and land) and others are functional (e.g., communications) or regional (e.g. Canadian Forces Europe). Where did the army go? Mostly, it now comes under Mobile Command, whose mission is "to maintain combat-ready land forces to meet Canada's varied defence commitments." Other army-type forces come under the regional or functional commands. Approximately forty per cent of Canada's 80,000 armed forces personnel could be classified as army, though Mobile Command itself has only 17,600 regular force personnel. (During both world wars the army alone reached a peak of more than 600,000).

The army's contribution to the direct defence of Canada during any emergency would be the weakest of the three "environmental" elements. Once fulfilled, the pledges we have made to NATO for troop reinforcements on its Central and Northern flanks would leave precisely two infantry battalions stationed in Canada – fewer than two thousand men charged with the land defence of half a continent. These troops would be immobilized because available military airlift capacity would be occupied meeting our European commitments.

To place this figure into the context of other emergencies: more than twice as many troops were involved in the 1970 October Crisis, and it is an astonishing admission of our military inadequacy that fewer than one-eighth of the troops required to patrol the grounds of the Montreal summer Olympic Games in 1976 are currently committed to the domestic defence of Canada should a Third World War ever break out.

The official rationale for this dismal state of affairs is that, because of our geography, we are not particularly vulnerable to direct land attack. This is not necessarily true. For one thing, a perceived threat can be as manpower-consuming as a real one. During the Second World War the sighting of a Japanese submarine off Canada's West Coast was considered a threat sufficient to justify keeping two army divisions at the ready in British Columbia for most of the duration.

One example of how troops can be massively tied down by relatively small threats: the British army uses more combat troops in Ulster against the IRA, which is estimated to have a hard-core combat strength of only 250 men, than the Canadian army possesses in total. Northern Ireland's six counties would fit tidily into the Ottawa Valley.

It might be argued that we have little to fear because Canada's regular army would be reinforced by the militia, which boasts a roll call of fifteen thousand, but according to Nicholas Stethem, executive director of the Strategic Analysis Group in Toronto, so many of the reservists are not eligible to go into battle that their front-line capability numbers fewer than a thousand infantrymen.

THE PRIDE OF THE CANADIAN ARMY is its 128 Leopard tanks, acquired in 1978. At any one time, forty-two of these machines are stationed in Canada, but it's a testimony to the military paltriness of this contingent that almost invariably there are simultaneously more German Leopard tanks (training with German troops at Shilo, Manitoba) and more Chieftain tanks (training with British troops at Suffield, Alberta) than there are Canadian tanks across the country.

Of the eighteen militia armoured regiments, none has a modern tank, and most have only a few Cougars (wheeled, as opposed to tracked, tank trainers) and a handful of battered jeeps. Other weapons are equally inadequate: the Italian 105mm pack howitzer is now fourteen years old and our C1-105mm guns have been in service since 1954. The army is in the process of switching from the twenty-seven-year-old, 7.62-millimetre FNC to a new rifle.

The highest estimate on what size a properly equipped standing army for Canada should be comes from Professor Philippe Garigue, principal of Glendon College at York University. A graduate of The Royal Military Academy at Sandhurst and a veteran of the Royal Fusiliers, he has called for immediate expansion to an army-in-being of three hundred thousand men and women. "Because of the present world situation, any conception that we have time to mobilize and develop a fully-trained Army within a given number of months or years is out of the question," he maintains.

It seems that an armed conflict may appear very rapidly and cannot be envisaged as the result of a long-changing deterioration which would give time for mobilization. We will have to fight with the forces that are then in existence. The notion that the Canadian Armed Forces is a cadre for a future expansion . . . is no longer valid. . . . In no case has any of the wars in the past twenty years been the result of an official declaration of war, nor did we have warning that there would be a given period of time before these wars did break out. You have to think of the present distribution of armed forces as those which will in fact do the fighting. You must think of a way of expanding to 300,000 immediately.

A more realistic assessment of current inadequacies comes from the Strategic Analysis Group's Nicholas Stethem:

Barring major collapse – a war in Europe or something like that – I do not see an increase in commitment for Canada, simply because unless we expanded our armed forces massively we could not meet those commitments. From what we do now, I suspect our allies would be satisfied if we did that job properly, which we do not. What we now do is not that far from what we did fifteen years ago, when we had a much larger armed force. We had roughly the same commitments. . . . The maintenance of a cosmetic ability, a "Let's-pretend" capability, fools no one except Canadians. Our allies know; they make no secret of it.

The most striking example of how undermanned (and under-gunned) the Canadian army has become is its mechanized brigade group on NATO's Central Front, at Lahr and Baden in West Germany. Unlike the Warsaw Pact troops which are maintained at ninety-five per cent of their war footing (against a NATO average of eighty-five per cent), Canada's contingent in Europe is kept at a bare fifty-eight per cent.

The Canadian troops have been assigned limited duty as reserves for counter-attack functions with the American 7th Army or the German 2nd Corps. The brigade cannot even defend itself. The airfields at Lahr and Baden are protected by hand-held Blowpipe missiles, little better than slingshots, and obsolete 40mm Bofors gun emplacements taken off the late and lamented HMCS *Bonaventure*.

Apart from the obsolescence of its scarce equipment, the very presence of Canadian troops on NATO's Central Front raises serious doubts. Many Western strategic analysts now believe that the classic threat that NATO was designed to meet – that of a massive Soviet blitzkrieg westward across the north German plain – has become one of the less likely fuses for an East-West collision. The Northern Gap, Middle East, and Persian Gulf are much more likely flash points.

ONE TOUCHY AREA OF DISCUSSION among Canada's defence planners is how our armed forces (particularly the army, or "land element") should be prepared to carry out internal security operations. The watchword here is that the military must always support and not supplant civil authority.

The historical roots of this controversial function stretch back to the withdrawal of the British Garrison in the years after Confederation, when responsibility for the maintenance of internal order fell to a fledgling federal government. The administration of justice became a local prerogative under the British North America Act, yet there was no adequate provincial or municipal constabulary in existence. The early militia acts were designed to allow various municipal authorities to call out the local defence forces to augment police resources when necessary. Commanding officers were required by law to respond, with volunteer officers and men, subject to fines if they didn't muster. It was also incumbent upon local commanders to recover from municipalities the costs of such intervention, and it was common for officers to bring personal lawsuits against city administrations to obtain their men's wages. Troops were used to maintain order on election days, at Orange Day parades, or to quell riots – even, on one occasion, to maintain order at a boxing match. During this early phase (until 1903) of internal security operations, the militia was called out on no less than seventy-two occasions for periods of service lasting up to six months.

In 1904 the first real amendment of the Militia Act was passed: municipalities were forced to provide a substantial financial deposit prior to the dispatch of troops; the small permanent force then in existence had to be called prior to the use of volunteer militia. The Crown would then undertake all actions to recover costs on behalf of individual commanding officers. From 1904 to 1940, particularly in the period before the First World War, the militia and the permanent force were called out to handle the protection of strike-breakers during union recognition battles and to restore order, especially in the coal mines of Cape Breton and Vancouver Island.

In 1924 a subtle but significant change, still in effect today, was made in the National Defence Act. It became necessary to have the provincial Attorney General, rather than municipal officials, sign military requisitions.

Since 1940 the Canadian army (and subsequently the Canadian Forces) have been involved in internal security operations twenty times. Four were ordered between 1940 and 1945 to support defence of Canadian regulations; eight arose due to riots in federal penitentiaries; and seven requisitions were from provinces. These included the Montreal police strike in 1969 and the October Crisis of 1970.

One of the many problems involved in this type of service was pointed out by Vice-Admiral Jock Allan when he was Deputy

Chief of Defence Staff. "The law, as it now stands," he told a Commons Committee,

> confers full peace officer status on all Canadian Forces personnel employed in internal security. This has certain advantages, such as powers of arrest and seizure, but also certain restrictions, specifically the individual responsibility to decide upon and apply only enough force to do the job. Therein lies the problem. Neither the status of peace officer nor the doctrine of minimum force are in themselves wrong. Policemen – full-time peace officers – are trained from the commencement of their career under these precepts, but soldiers are not. Soldiers must realize they will be accountable for their actions. The differences in training, organization, responsibility, command structure, and philosophy in the professional use of arms are too great to allow a good soldier to be a good policeman. Each is a full-time job. Indeed, to fully train a soldier in the restraint and individual actions necessary for police tasks would obviously detract from his abilities as a soldier.

Just how theoretical all of this postulating can remain will depend on the evolution of Canadian history. In September 1978, a report from London's Institute for the Study of Conflict was prepared by Major-General Rowland Mans, a British officer who had spent three years with the Canadian Army Staff College in Kingston, Ontario. It warned with dramatic clarity of the risks inherent in a potentially disunited Canada. "Just how long the United States would be prepared to stand idly by if the situation worsened would be a matter of nice judgment," Mans wrote. And he concluded, "Traditional Canadian complacency, the open society, and a feeling generated by its geography that 'it can't happen here,' help to create the troubled waters in which the revolutionary fish can swim and propagate."

The former director-general of the RCMP Security Service, John Starnes, wrote in a 1977 issue of the British magazine, *Survival*, that "Canada's international situation is such that, for the first time since NATO was formed, there is now a potential threat to the security of the North American heartland." Two years before the FLQ crisis, Prime Minister Pierre Trudeau told a Queen's University student questioner: "I happen to believe that in a very real sense civilization and culture in North America are more menaced by internal disorders than by external pressure." Trudeau emphasized he envisaged a North America with "large rebellions and large disturbances of civil order."

Canada does have a Special Services Force, thirty-five-hundred-men strong, described as being "airportable and airdroppable." Officially it is designated as a reinforcement unit for our NATO contingent and peacekeeping units, but as Roy MacGregor wrote in *Maclean's*: "There will be those who wonder why the Forces have 2,500 pairs of handcuffs and 17,800 gas masks despite the fact that no Canadian soldier has come under gas attack since 1918." He also observed that some fifty special armoured vehicles were at the Petawawa base, "vehicles that as well as their military uses, are nearly identical to those employed by the West German police and others for riot control. Such items are dismissed as basic equipment by the defence department, though one critic has said they 'fit better into the needs of unstable banana republics' than those of Canada."

CHAPTER SEVEN

Without a Parachute

There is at present, no radar coverage along the northern coast of British Columbia, nor along the East Coast from Cape Dyer to Goose Bay. These corridors into Canadian air space remain unguarded, almost inviting attack.

C ANADA IS THE ONLY COUNTRY IN THE WORLD whose air force is larger than its army.* In this space age, it is equipped with a wild assortment of twenty-three different types of aircraft – most of which date back to the 1960s and earlier.

The air force's main combat aircraft are the twenty-two-year-old, CF-104 Starfighters stationed at Baden in West Germany. The planes have virtually no effective air-to-air defence capabilities, are limited to daylight visual operations, and only half of them are kept on station anyway. The 1st Canadian Air Group is composed of three squadrons for a total of fifty-four aircraft, plus five in reserve. But, unlike its army counterpart, the air force's NATO contribution is maintained at fifty-eight per cent of its strength, with only thirty-six aircraft manned on a full-time basis. The crews of the others would be expected to make it over from Cold Lake, Alberta, if, as the flyboys are so fond of saying, "the balloon goes up."

The other major fighting contingent of the air force is commit-

*This is partly accounted for by the fact that the Air Command of the Canadian Forces includes such elements as the army's tactical helicopters and the navy's destroyer-based helicopters, as well as the department's search-and-rescue operations, which in other countries are not part of the military. Despite the large number of personnel, Lieutenant-General George Allan MacKenzie, who retired as the head of Air Command in 1980, has estimated that the service is short of nearly 400 key technicians and navigators.

ted to NORAD, currently manned by CF-101 Voodoos, which went into service in 1961. Most of these planes are older than the men who fly them.

This sad state of obsolescence is changing as the first of the 138 McDonnell Douglas CF-18 Hornets come into service. Delivery of the $4-billion order has been stretched out for budgetary reasons, so that the first full squadron will not become operational until late in 1984 and the last plane won't be delivered until four years after that. Eighty-four of the CF-18s will be stationed in North America, most of them attached to NORAD, part of Canada's defence arrangements since 1957.

The original NORAD Agreement (it is not, strictly speaking, a military alliance) grew out of the fears generated by the explosion of the USSR's first nuclear bomb in 1949. Canada and the United States decided to build the Pinetree Radar Line in 1951, the Mid-Canada Line in 1954, and the Distant Early Warning (DEW) Line in 1955. The North American Air Defense Command, agreed to two years later, was to become the most expensive force in military history ever committed solely to a defence function. All the wizardry and ingenuity of modern electronics have gone into trying to perfect NORAD's air warning net. About 56,500 personnel (approximately 10,400 of them Canadians) man the detection and defence system, which covers nearly eleven million square miles of air space. Its territory stretches from the polar ice cap to the Mexican border.

Between 1958 and 1962 NORAD perfected its anti-bomber system to the point that its commanders felt able to claim that there could be no surprise air attack on North America. During this period the DEW Line was completed and linked up with similar radar coverage in Iceland and the United Kingdom. The Mid-Canada and Pinetree lines were supplemented with additional radar sites scattered throughout the United States. Long-range early warning aircraft, U.S. Navy picket ships, dirigibles, and U.S. Air Force Texas towers were placed on permanent stations to ensure protection against "end run" tactics from either the Atlantic or Pacific.

NORAD's most significant scientific success was its Ballistic Missile Early Warning System (BMEWS) which, in an eighth of a

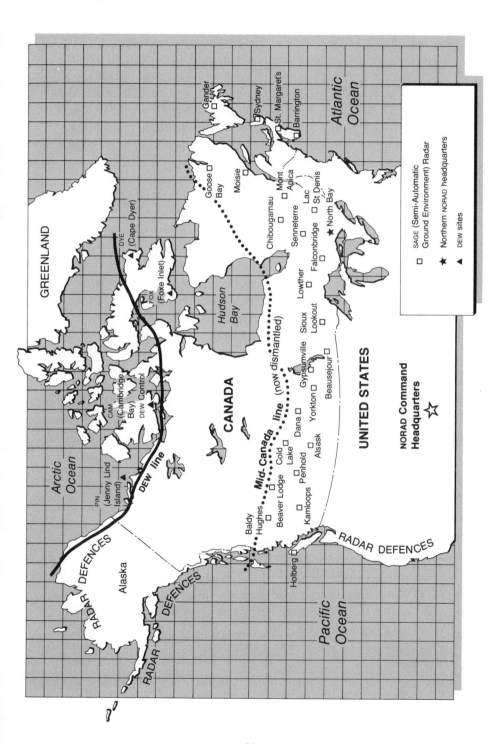

GREENLAND

Arctic Ocean

Atlantic Ocean

Pacific Ocean

Hudson Bay

CANADA

UNITED STATES

Alaska

RADAR DEFENCES
RADAR DEFENCES
RADAR DEFENCES
RADAR DEFENCES

DEW line

DEW Control

Mid-Canada line (now dismantled)

NORAD Command Headquarters ☆

Gander
Sydney
St. Margaret's
Barrington
Goose Bay
Moisie
Mont. Apica
Lac
St Denis
Chibougamau
Senneterre
Falconbridge
★ North Bay
Lowther
Sioux Lookout
Gypsumville
Yorkton
Beausejour
Dana
Cold Lake
Alsask
Penhold
Baldy Hughes
Beaver Lodge
Kamloops
Holberg

DYE (Cape Dyer)
FOX (Foxe Inlet)
CAM (Cambridge Bay)
PIN (Jenny Lind Island)

□ SAGE (Semi-Automatic Ground Environment) Radar
□ Northern NORAD headquarters
★ Northern NORAD headquarters
▲ DEW sites

63

second, can spot ICBMs rising over the horizon three thousand miles away. The first of these radar installations, 600 miles north of the Arctic Circle at Thule, Greenland, came into operation on October 1, 1960. The others are located at Clear, Alaska, and Fylingdales Moor, Yorkshire, England. Between them, these radar antennas – each the size of a football field tipped on its side – will detect missiles rising anywhere in the Eurasian land mass. (They operate by radiating twin fans of radar energy at different elevations. The lower-level fan can detect an object the moment it sticks over the horizon, while the upper fan gives details for the calculation of the missile's trajectory. An electronic computer instantly flashes this calculation to NORAD headquarters at Colorado Springs, giving the missile's probable destination and time of impact.)

For the past two decades, NORAD has operated a network to detect space vehicles through techniques known as "Spacetrack" and the "Naval Space Surveillance System." Spacetrack is a world-wide network of high-powered radars and Baker-Nunn cameras which identify and catalogue man-made objects in orbit around the earth. (One of the Baker-Nunn camera sites is at St. Margaret's, New Brunswick.) The Naval Space Surveillance System is made up of three transmitter and six receiver sites located across the southern United States. Because of the number of man-made objects currently in orbit and because the potential military threat requires more timely information than can be supplied by the Baker-Nunn cameras, a new system known as Ground-Based Electro-Optical Deep Space Surveillance has been developed to replace Spacetrack. No sites are projected for Canada. The new system is already tracking the five-thousand-plus man-made objects now orbiting the planet – including the glove lost by a perambulating astronaut.

Since 1962, technological advances have reduced the DEW Line from 70 sites to 31, the Mid-Canada Line has been dismantled, and the Pinetree Line and American continental radar installations have been reduced from 256 to 80. All surface radar picket ships, dirigibles, and Texas towers have been scrapped; early-warning aircraft capability has been reduced to minimal levels; surface-to-air missile formations (like the controversial Bomarc)

64

have been scrapped; the number of fighter/interceptors under NORAD command has been cut from 1,600 to 517.

According to a recent report in *The Financial Post*, the current DEW Line stations will be replaced with a mixture of fifteen manned, long-range radar positions and thirty-five robot-stations with short-range capacities. This $600-million DEW Line refitting is the first phase of an eventual $7.6 billion-plus program. According to American estimates, Canada will pay $429 million (in U.S. dollars) versus the Pentagon's $3.4 billion for NORAD's upkeep during 1983, and an as yet undetermined share of the ultimate modernization costs.

With a land-based ICBM flight time from the Soviet Union of less than thirty minutes (and not even half that time for a ballistic missile launched from an offshore submarine), warning intervals have become NORAD's most critical assignment.

First warning of a ballistic missile attack would come from three satellites equipped with infra-red sensors in geosynchronous orbit. In the final testing stage is the Over-the-Horizon Backscatter radar system designed to provide long range (up to two thousand miles), all-altitude coverage. It will cover the east and west coasts of North America but a northern employment is not feasible because of interference from the aurora borealis.

Providing back-up for a large part of the BMEWS coverage is a phased-array radar (PARS) located near Concrete, North Dakota, with a range of 1,800 nautical miles. (It's the surviving element of the ABM system, dismantled after SALT-I.) It is supplemented by the Sea-Launched Ballistic Missile Detection and Warning System, with radars and sonars located on the east, west, and Gulf coasts of the United States.

The DEW Line ground-based radar stations extend their coverage from northwest Alaska to eastern Greenland, but significant gaps exist. There is, at present, no radar coverage along the northern coast of British Columbia, nor along the East Coast from Cape Dyer to Goose Bay. These corridors into Canadian air space remain unguarded, almost inviting attack.

DESPITE THE EFFORTS TO BRING NORAD into the space age, the

Command's defensive facilities are all designed to meet the threat of the manned bomber. Every commercial plane that approaches North America or flies over certain zones comes under NORAD scrutiny, and, in some cases, if the plane is as little as ten miles off its previously-filed flight plan, a NORAD fighter may be scrambled to identify it visually.

These fighters are part of NORAD's defense "wall" of twenty squadrons of fighter/interceptors – which includes thirty-six Canadian CF-101s. But the state of readiness is so low that at the moment only four planes are kept at the five-minute readiness alert required by contemporary defence measures. (Two of these Voodoos are at Bagotville, Quebec, and two at Comox, British Columbia.)

Although Canada pays only eight per cent of NORAD's annual bill, its aircraft remain under national jurisdiction and can be brought to full alert only with the concurrence of Canada's prime minister. (During neither the 1962 Cuban missile showdown nor the 1973 Middle East crisis did the Canadian government officially sanction the higher priority. The Americans have since designated their own officers to move into Canadian NORAD functions, should such circumstances recur.)

In an age when the balance of intercontinental missiles has become the chief strategic consideration, it's valid to wonder why such an elaborate and expensive system must be maintained against the possibility of bomber attacks. Between 1962 and 1982 the Soviets reduced their long-range Bear and Bison bomber fleets from 225 to 126, while the numbers of their medium-range aircraft (Badgers and Blinders) went down from 700 to 630 – although aerial refuelling capacity was added to turn these planes into possible intercontinental weapons. What makes the NORAD anti-bomber commitment necessary is that the USSR has started building new long-range Backfire bombers armed with stand-off missiles. About a hundred of these new jets are already in service and they are reported to be coming off production lines at the rate of three per month. It's estimated that fifteen per cent of the Soviets' nuclear "payload" is currently mounted on bombers.

The USSR is known to be planning a new, long-range variable-wing bomber, known as the Blackjack-A. It will probably act as a carrier of cruise missiles. What little is known about the Blackjack comes from the sighting of a prototype at an airstrip outside Moscow in 1981.

The substitution of the new CF-18* for the outdated CF-101s and CF-104s will give Canada not only a modern interceptor on domestic station charged with home defence, but the range and capacity of the new interceptors will allow the air force the potential to exercise Canadian sovereignty in our northern airspace. At the same time, the substitution will remove the last of the nuclear warheads in use by the Canadian Forces – the air-to-air nuclear-tipped Genie missiles used by the Voodoos will be replaced by conventionally armed Sidewinders or Sparrows.

At the moment, because of our NATO commitments, the number of CF-18s remaining on this side of the Atlantic would be limited to three squadrons, or fifty-four planes, stationed at Cold Lake, Alberta, and Bagotville, Quebec.

This is a false division of resources. The planes might or might not have time (or safe passage) to reach their NATO positions. Even if they did, their addition would not influence the size of NATO's overall deterrent. The Alliance currently has 2,975 ground-attack fighters deployed in Europe. No other Allied air force stationed in Europe will be using F-18s, so that the three Canadian squadrons would be limited to their home airfield for servicing.

Rather than their marginal use in NATO, all of Canada's new CF-18 interceptors should be added to strengthen the Canadian contribution to the North American Aerospace Defence Command, particularly in view of the fact that the Soviet Union is developing both new long-range bombers and cruise-type missiles. We should therefore station all of the new CF-18s in Canada, reducing our reliance on American air power.

THERE IS ANOTHER PRACTICAL WAY in which Canada could con-

---

*Under the terms of the $2.4 billion contract signed with the U.S. in 1980, Canada agreed to buy 138 of the CF-18s over a seven-year period from McDonnell Douglas Corp. of St. Louis, Missouri. The aircraft's development costs totalled an astounding $38 billion. In exchange, the American firm agreed to provide Canadian industry with $2.9 billion worth of orders between 1977 and 1995.

tribute to its own defence. While we should not try to add to the West's nuclear retaliatory element, we must do all we can to identify precisely what is happening over Canada, one of the world's most strategically vital airspaces. The best way to do this would be to purchase (or better still, to manufacture) at least half a dozen Airborne Warning and Control System (AWACS) aircraft.

Because of the gaps in radar surveillance caused over Canada by interference from the aurora borealis, only AWACS aircraft (which are really flying radar stations) can provide the kind of foolproof surveillance that strengthens the credibility of a deterrent. Describing why the air defence of North America needs AWACS, Admiral J. C. Edwards told a Parliamentary Committee:

> At the present time, Soviet bombers could underfly the radar detection coverage provided by both the Dew Line and the Pinetree networks. Soviet bombers could penetrate Canadian airspace undetected along the East and West coasts where no radar coverage now exists. The Soviet Backfire could fly through the high altitude radar surveillance coverage of either the Dew Line or the Pinetree chain in about fifteen minutes. The existing radars and associated communications systems are not hardened or protected and could be disabled without too much difficulty. Lastly, the ROCCs will only have a limited wartime capability. The full extent of Canadian participation in AWACS is yet to be determined. However, because the NORAD AWACS must provide warning and control as far North as possible, our involvement is considered to be highly desirable, both from the point of view of our continued support of the NORAD systems, and to maintain some level of control of AWACS operations when the system operates in Canadian airspace.

AWACS can survey about eight hundred square miles at a time, moving at eight miles a minute at an altitude of forty thousand feet.* Adoption of the AWACS by Canada's armed forces would cause no great technical problems. NATO maintains its own fleet of AWACS at Geilenkirchen in West Germany, and, even though it's

---

*The USSR has developed its own version of the AWACS. Known as the "MOSS," it is a converted Tupolev-126 and there are at least a dozen already in the air.

not well-known, we already contribute $200 million a year for the acquisition of these planes. Approximately 140 Canadian servicemen are part of their regular in-flight and support crews; other Canadians are involved with the NORAD fleet of twenty-five AWACS, operating out of the American Air Force base at Tinker, Oklahoma. The AWACS make regular calls to Canadian airfields and are already over-flying Canadian airspace.

It costs about $150 million to buy a complete AWACS. One cost-cutting possibility suggests itself. Though the bulk of our AWACS fleet would have to be kept on permanent station at forward bases in Frobisher, Cold Lake, Whitehorse, Goose Bay, North Bay, and Resolute, should the AWACS require permanent southern basing quarters – what better use for the semi-deserted runways at Mirabel?

Such a fleet of high-altitude observation planes would give us an effective eye on what's happening in our own country.

CHAPTER EIGHT

The Vanishing Reserves

In 1936, when the Calgary Regiment became Canada's First Reserve Tank Unit, burlap-covered frames on motorcycles were its first "tanks" – until they were replaced by sheet-metal-covered Chevrolets.

I N ANY COMPARISON of the ratio between regular and reserve military manpower in the world's industrialized countries, Canada ranks right at the very bottom.

Outside NATO, such neutral countries as Sweden (population: 8.3 million, number of reservists: 656,500), Switzerland (population: 6.3 million, number of reservists: 621,500), and Austria (population: 7.5 million, number of reservists: 960,000) maintain impressive back-up capabilities. West Germany can mobilize three-quarters of a million fighting men within three days. About sixty per cent of France's navy is made up of short-term personnel who begin their tours of duty after only a two-week training period.

The Soviet Union maintains an estimated five million reservists; the United States has fewer than one million. Perhaps Norway displays the most remarkable example of how a small nation supplements its readiness for emergencies: with a population of only four million, it can field a home guard of 247,000 at a moment's notice – though their quality has been called into question.

Here is how Canada – with fewer than 19,000 under-trained and under-equipped reservists – compares with other NATO members:

71

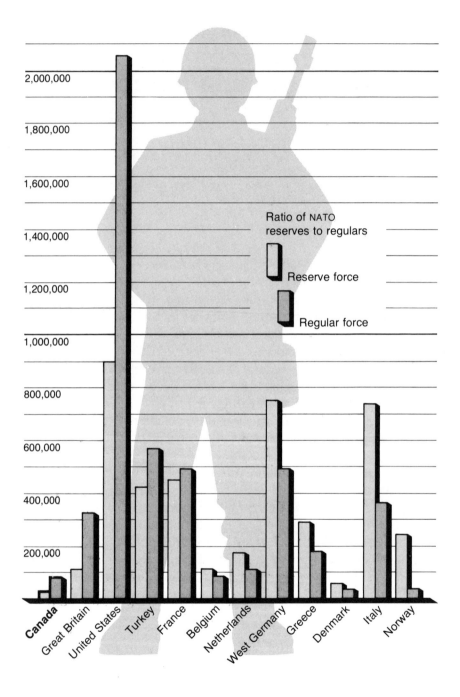

2,000,000			
1,800,000			
1,600,000			
1,400,000		Ratio of NATO reserves to regulars	
1,200,000		Reserve force	
1,000,000		Regular force	
800,000			
600,000			
400,000			
200,000			

Canada Great Britain United States Turkey France Belgium Netherlands West Germany Greece Denmark Italy Norway

It was not always so.

Canada's military reserves have a proud and long tradition – their roots go back to the seventeenth century. They were first established for the defence of New France against the colonists of New England. French- and English-Canadian militiamen supported the British army, standing side by side against the Americans. The York Volunteers participated with Brock at Queenston Heights, and the greatly outnumbered Voltigeurs fought under Charles de Salaberry along the Chateauguay in the War of 1812. From these and other actions came our strong belief in the ability of the militia to protect the nation. It was not until the withdrawal of the British garrisons in 1870 and 1871 that Canada raised any regulars of its own.

Canada's modern reserve force originated in the Militia Act of 1855, which established a five-thousand-man volunteer force of cavalry, artillery, and infantry. Because of tensions resulting from the American Civil War in the early 1860s and the Fenian raids later that decade, this troop had been expanded to forty thousand by the early 1870s.

Throughout the decades up to the First World War, the militia maintained a steady program of officer training, with regular instruction from visiting British senior officers. This program, which traditionally involved the social elite of the country, undoubtedly put the country in a better position than might have been expected to raise an exceptionally effective army at the time of the war.

By the eve of the First World War, the carefully nurtured regimental system was discarded in favour of a hastily developed mobilization plan. The militia provided the platform on which was raised an army of more than 619,000 officers and men in a country with a population in 1914 of only eight million. (Of these, 418,000 served overseas; nearly 60,000 were killed.)

The first post-war reorganization of the militia was prompted by the Otter Committee, formed in 1919. The old pre-war regiments did not wish to give up their identities, and the new Canadian Expeditionary Force regiments, which had fought and suffered in the trenches, did not want to be assimilated by them. In the end, nearly all the units of the pre-First World War militia lost their titles. The committee based its manning recommendations on a militia strength of four cavalry and eleven infantry divisions, plus supporting services – a total of 135,000 men. This unrealistically large force was called for by a defence plan which supposed that Canada was in danger of invasion from the United States. By 1931, the "non-permanent active militia," as it was then called, had an actual strength of 51,000 men.

In 1936, the second reorganization was aimed at developing and training a force of one cavalry (armour) and six infantry divisions as a practical Canadian contribution to the British Commonwealth in the event of another overseas war. By 1938, the strength of the peacetime militia had been set at 86,000, although actual strength was about half that. The limitations on equipment have a familiar ring: in 1936, when the Calgary Regiment became Canada's First Reserve Tank Unit, burlap-covered frames on motorcycles were its first "tanks" – until they were replaced by sheet-metal-covered Chevrolets.

After the Second World War the post-war Canadian Army Reserves were divided into five sub-components: the reserve force, the supplementary reserve, the Canadian Officer Training Corps (COTC), the cadet services of Canada, and the reserve militia. Within this reorganization, reserve establishments were based on four armoured brigade and six infantry divisions plus anti-aircraft artillery and a number of home defence units on both coasts.

THE ROYAL NAVAL CANADIAN VOLUNTEER RESERVE (RNCVR) began as an unpaid group at Victoria, British Columbia, in 1913. Before it was disbanded after the First World War it provided sailors for service in the British fleet and on the Canadian East Coast.

Facing severe cuts in defence budgets in the early 1920s, the Director of Naval Service decided to dispose of half his regular establishments, close the naval college – and raise a series of naval reserve units in cities from coast to coast to maintain a visible naval presence. His foresight allowed the navy's manpower to be expanded in 1939 when war was declared, growing to more than fifty times its peacetime strength and permitting the navy to carry the burden of defending the North Atlantic.

At the same time, the Naval Reserve, in the form established between the wars, was maintained, although like the other components of the reserve forces, its strength steadily declined.

IN 1920, THE CANADIAN AIR FORCE (CAF), a non-permanent organization, was formed to give former Royal Flying Corps pilots and ground crews month-long refresher courses every second year. Four years later, the CAF had developed into the Royal Canadian Air Force. During the depression years, the RCAF suffered major budgetary cuts, and by 1939 there were only about three thousand personnel in the regular RCAF and one thousand in the RCAF auxiliary. This provided a three-wing headquarters and twelve squadrons, which became the nucleus for the early RCAF contribution to the wartime defence effort. Eventually the RCAF grew to 250,000 personnel.

At the end of the Second World War, the RCAF resumed its roles in aerial photography, survey, and air transport. In 1946 it was reorganized on the basis of a regular force of eight squadrons and an air auxiliary force of fifteen squadrons. For a dozen years the air auxiliary continued to expand until by 1958 it had reached a maximum strength of 6,000. Over the next sixteen years the air reserve went through a series of cuts and restructurings until it was down to only 580 personnel, supporting six squadrons of single-engine Otter aircraft in four Canadian cities.

DURING THE PERIOD OF THE COLD WAR, nuclear weapons increasingly dominated defence policies, and incidentally produced a revolutionary rearrangement in the relationship of reserves to regulars. The regulars, vastly outnumbered by the part-timers, had traditionally supplied a small cadre of professionals to train reserves, who were counted on to provide the necessary flesh and muscle in emergencies. Since the Second World War, the regulars have exceeded the reserves in number, with reservists being vaguely considered an auxiliary force.

The "forces-in-being" concept propagated in the 1964 Canadian government White Paper was predicated on the theme of a short, sharp, intensive war, with no time to mobilize, in which nuclear weapons would be employed. Under these circumstances there was little requirement for reserves and it seemed a waste of time and money to prepare for a situation in which they were unlikely to be used. The result was that the reserves were left to languish, and the whole notion of mobilization planning was lost by default.

Now that a longer conventional-type war has become an option, a "total-force" concept has re-emerged. It postulates that both the primary and supplementary reserves, in partnership with the regular force, would be required in any major emergency, but the Canadian government has yet to acknowledge this fundamental concept as far as its policy towards the reserves is concerned. At present only 3.9% of the defence budget (about $250 million) goes towards the reserves – consisting of a dedicated but forgotten few.

The naval reserve is divided into divisions in eighteen cities across the country from HMCS *Malahat* in Victoria to HMCS *Cabot* at St. John's. An integral part of Maritime Command, their purpose is to augment the regular force and to staff completely, if mobilized, the Naval Control of Shipping Organization. Turnover in personnel is about eighty per cent every two years. Training problems were outlined to the House of Commons External Affairs and National Defence Committee recently by W. N. Fox-Decent, a professor of political science at the University of Manitoba, who was later promoted to Chief of Naval Reserves:

> The buildings are essentially barren barns full of ancient and obsolete pieces of equipment which do not relate, even to our ancient destroyers. We are talking about 35- and 45-year-old equipment, almost all of which does not function. There is nobody who knows how to fix it any more, and we cannot get the parts anyway. . . .We will live with our 25-year-old North Sea trawlers. They are great little ships, they really are, but they will eventually rust out, and you can only put so many plugs in the bottom before they can no longer be used. They have not reached that stage yet, but they soon will.

Fox-Decent's predecessor, Rear-Admiral Tom Smith, told the same Parliamentary Committee:

> Sometimes I wonder how our reserves have held on over the

years, because there has been an attempt to stamp them out, like everything else. Perhaps a better expression for it would be a kind of educated neglect. . . .Our troops are also our children. They come from the most elaborate, well-equipped schools and on entering the forces find they have to work with some of the most antiquated equipment you ever saw.* If you want to feel ashamed, go into some of our establishments. We have a national scandal on our hands: the reserves.

When he was asked the precise vintage of the diesel engines used by reserve units for training, Admiral Smith wouldn't say, except to admit that most of them have given out. "There is a vigil light in front of them," he quipped.

The militia have fared no better. In 1972, all militia units, with the exception of eleven signal units, were placed under Mobile Command. These reserves are organized into five geographic areas – Atlantic, Eastern, Central, Prairie, and Pacific – each commanded by a brigadier general. These 5 area headquarters control, in turn, some 22 district headquarters, each of which is commanded by a colonel. The organizational thread unwinds further to encompass 136 units, grouped geographically at 111 locations. Current policy assigns to the militia the individual augmentation of regular force units in an emergency and the provision of a base for subsequent expansion. In the case of the militia – and only in the case of the militia – these two requirements are considered mutually exclusive.

The most damning indictment of the state of the army's reserves before the recent Parliamentary Committee on the subject came from Louis Desmarais, a Liberal Member of Parliament who belongs to a militia unit in Quebec:

We have a lack of equipment that is basically unbelievable. We have 150 young militiamen in our unit and only 75 rifles, so they are sharing rifles. How do you like that! This is a soldier, and we

*One skipper of the *Porte St. Jean*, (launched in 1951 and condemned as unseaworthy on her maiden voyage), recently felt so ashamed of his gate vessel that he went to a Canadian Tire store and purchased enough material to build a wooden gun on her forecastle. Using a narrow-gauge open sewer pipe as a barrel, he painted the whole contraption grey and ran up some empty Javex bottles on her mast to simulate the style of fire-direction electronics that would make the tub look more like a warship.

cannot even supply him with his own rifle to look after. Ammunition: on these exercises we have to simulate ammunition by asking the guys to say, "bang, bang!" – as you did when you were 12 years old behind a building.* It becomes ridiculous. Clothing: there is only one set of clothing. We asked these fellows to wear the same boots, the same trousers, the same everything for a whole week – mud, rain, sun, whatever, it is just one pair, and that is it. We have a jeep and it is never working, there is always something wrong with it. . . . .The cost-of-living allowance has been forgotten somewhere in some kind of paper work, because we cannot even afford a Big Mac for our people.

The degree of actual mobilization readiness of the militia units is a topic of lively debate. An article in the Winter 1979 edition of the *Canadian Defence Quarterly* claimed that of the 5,817 infantrymen in the militia at that time, only 647 would be available to augment the regular force. The remainder consisted of recruits, students, female support personnel, underage recruits, or those working in essential occupations. At the moment reservists in Canada can not be called to duty in an emergency unless they specifically volunteer.

The air reserve consists of two wings (in Montreal and Toronto), and three small squadrons (in Edmonton, Winnipeg, and Summerside), performing operational activities alongside the regular force and providing direct augmentation for regular force units. Their quality is high but their quantity is pitiful. In an age of space, the entire air reserves totals 950 personnel, 100 of whom are trained pilots. Their only up-to-date piece of equipment is the Kiowa helicopter, the same aircraft that is used for city traffic reports by radio stations. The Dakotas flown by the Winnipeg squadron were designed in 1935 and built in 1942.

The communication reserve, formed in 1972 from the eleven signal units of the old militia, now numbers 1,560, with an annual turnover of thirty per cent.

There is also the surprisingly vital para-military cadet program

*There is a continually retold, apocryphal story about two recruits confronting each other with broomsticks. One yells: "You've had it, man. I shot you with this rifle." "No you didn't," is the reply. "I'm a tank."

comprising 5,400 officers and 59,000 cadets in 1,040 corps across the country.

The only other element of the reserves is the corps of Canadian Rangers. Each member of this 650-man Indian and Inuit formation is issued a rifle, an identifying arm band, and 100 rounds of ammunition, replenished yearly. They are vaguely ordered to report any "foreign" activity along their traplines. Being wise to Ottawa's self-deceptions, they do the only sensible thing: use the free ammunition to hunt animals and forget the rest of the white man's silly games.

THE RELATIONSHIP BETWEEN RESERVES AND REGULAR FORCES, especially at staff level, is difficult at the best of times. With reserves as pathetically reduced as they are, it is not surprising that the regular forces seem reluctant to delegate them any policy-planning function. This was most forcefully described by Major-General Richard Rohmer, who served as Canada's Chief of Reserves for three years:

> During my tenure, the Chief of the Defence Staff never asked me anything at all. I did not fault him because I would go to him and tell him what I thought, so there was a good relationship. I waited for the phone to ring and have the Chief at the other end of the phone saying, "General, what do you think about this in relation to the reserves?" The phone never rang. . . .
> I went to the Chief of the Defence Staff, of my own volition, about two and one half years ago and said: "Chief, there is no plan for the utilization of the reserve forces on A-Day" – A-Day being Alert Day, when somebody pushes the button and we go, which is the reason for having an armed force, let alone a reserve force. I said, "There is no plan whereby the reserve force knows what it is supposed to do on A-Day, so that the regiment in Galt, or Guelph, or the regiments in the Maritimes know what they are supposed to do." He said, "My gracious." So, as a result of that, I was tasked to attempt to work with the commanders of the various commands to come up with an immediate reaction plan for the reserve force. I worked at this for a

while and I very quickly discovered that not only was there no plan for the reserve force, but there was no plan for the regular force for its own response. As a result, two years ago, the then Deputy Chief of Defence Staff put a task force together to prepare a plan for mobilization. They produced a plan all right, and just before I retired, a preliminary document was prepared and circulated. I want to tell you that by the time I had left the office of Chief of Reserves the mobilization task force people had never talked to the reserve force once in the preparation of the plan, although we had said we were prepared to advise and give our views, because much of this plan has to do with the reserve force.

THE DOWNGRADING OF CANADA'S RESERVES has a lot to do with the fact that sometime during the 1960s, the country's social establishment deserted them, as it also deserted Royal Military College and Royal Roads for university-level education. For the previous half century and more, it had been "fashionable" to join the historic regiments, and to a lesser but still significant extent, local air force and naval reserve units. These acted in a very real way as the Establishment's finishing schools. But the attractiveness of alternate challenges, the laughable lack of adequate equipment, the "civil defence" aspects of the weekly parades – these and other factors prompted the Establishment's scions to seek other outlets for their time and energy. With their departure, the reserves lost much of their political clout, and the visible support of any sector of Canadian society.

One sure sign of the decline of the reserves is the low regard with which they are now held by the community-at-large. T. C. Willett, a professor of sociology at Queen's University, recently undertook a three-year study of Canada's militia reserves. His conclusion was that

the units seem to have become virtual non-entities in their communities, and their once prominent civic role has almost disappeared. While there is no evident hostility towards them, ignorance and apathy are marked. The once close relationship

80

between units, civic leaders, and such organizations as the Royal Canadian Legion has weakened, and it is common to find mayors and police chiefs whose contacts with the Militia are confined to occasional visits on formal occasions which do little to show what the unit does or could do. Because of severe limits in the number of paid days, public appearances are limited to one church parade and November 11th ceremonies, in contrast with the monthly, or even weekly public displays of an earlier period. Mostly, units train inside armouries or in the country where they are not on public view.

Expressing similar doubts, Douglas Fisher, the newspaper columnist and a veteran of the Normandy landings in the Second World War, has described "a system of reserve forces that is laughable – a catch-as-catch-can, scattered set of understrength units, distinguished by high turnover, brief engagements, and old-fashioned equipment."

The former Chief of Defence Staff Ramsay Withers reiterated the essential function of the reserves before the Parliamentary Committee recently:

The whole basis of our strategy in the NATO alliance is one of deterrence. It is one of preventing war through credible forces that can meet the threat that exists across the whole spectrum. We must have an effective reserve system. We do not talk about this very often, but the value of effective reserves is the message they can give, diplomatically. One of the very low cost, but nonetheless important, messages you can transmit international-ly, is to call out your reserves. Indeed, if one examines history, one sees that this has been used effectively to cause individuals to think twice, and not proceed to conflict. Of course, to do that you must have effective reserves; it cannot be an empty signal, it has to be a reasonable one. In a national sense, it is an impor-tant message to transmit in any time of emergency because it clearly shows your citizens a serious situation that has to be attended to – even taking the step of not actually recalling reserves, but putting reserves on notice of recall. It is important to think about this in Canada because our reserves are the very roots of the country.

CHAPTER NINE

Taming the Nuclear Demon

"The nuclear arms race has no military purpose. Wars cannot be fought with atomic weapons."
EARL MOUNTBATTEN OF BURMA

WHEN DR. BARRY HUNT, a Canadian historian who teaches at the Royal Military College in Kingston, Ontario, was testifying before a recent Senate Committee on Defence, he was asked about the uses of nuclear weapons in future wars. "I must admit to you, quite frankly," he replied, "that when one opens up debate on that subject, my mind turns to mush. I find it difficult to be logical when considering what would take place."

The professor's hesitation is understandable: few contemporary issues command more emotion and less enlightenment.

Anyone in his right mind must favour nuclear disarmament. But for any superpower to give up voluntarily the one weapon which inspires the degree of fear necessary to deter aggression – that kind of unilateral surrender requires an act of faith hardly justified by current circumstances.

The longing for peace and all those dreams of mutual brotherhood that humanity craves remain as elusive as ever. Barbara Tuchman, whose epic studies of war have made her an expert in recognizing the sequence of blunders that lead men into battle, has declared herself to be skeptical about the attainment of peace. "Peace," she writes,

> has not figured among the notable achievements of mankind. It is the most talked of and least practiced of all social endeavours. Men – and in this case I mean the male gender, not the species – are always saying they hate war and war is hell and so forth, and

yet have continued to engage in it lustily, aggressively and ceaselessly since the beginning of recorded history, and doubtless before. Historians have estimated that society has spent more time fighting than in any other activity except agriculture. Sumerians, Babylonians and Assyrians, Egyptians and Israelites, Greeks and Romans, Scythians, Carthaginians, Huns and Goths, Mongols and Turks, Celts and Saxons, Europeans and Americans, Chinese, Japanese and Moslems have fought each other or among themselves or against some opponent at every stage of civilization. Peace is brief, as fragile and transitory as apple blossoms in the spring.

Disarmament efforts in the twentieth century were heralded by the first Hague Peace Conference in 1899, prompted by public fear of the swelling armaments industry. The summons to this world conference, and its successor in 1907, issued by Czar Nicholas II, who was lagging behind in the arms race, surpassed the wildest dreams of the advocates of peace, sounding, in the words of a Viennese newspaper editorial, "like beautiful music over the whole earth." The conference's results were carefully tailored to distress no war departments and nothing done at The Hague restrained the Balkan Wars from breaking out, nor the explosion of the First World War.

The battered nations that emerged from that "war to end all wars" made a serious effort towards world order through formation of the League of Nations and the Permanent Court of International Justice.

Despite much talk and endless international posturing, only one effective act of arms control was signed in the two decades that followed. The Washington Naval Conference of 1922 achieved an agreement by the United States, Great Britain, and Japan to a limitation on battleships in the ratio of 5:5:3, and an agreement on nonfortification of the Pacific islands. But because Japan furiously resented holding the short end of the 5:5:3 ratio, the effect of the treaties was ultimately negated. Resentment fueled the rising Japanese militarism that eventually led to the attack on Pearl Harbor. When the League of Nations blamed Japan – as politely as possible – for the invasion of Manchuria, Japan departed from

Geneva and officially repudiated the 1922 naval agreement. Germany left the League six months later, denounced the Versailles Treaty – and launched its own rearmament program. Its troops reoccupied the Rhineland while Italy invaded Ethiopia in a challenge that the League powers failed to meet even by sanctions. Collective security became a moribund concept and the escalation that led to the Second World War was set in motion.

Yet again, men fought a "war to end all wars," but this time with a difference: the nuclear holocausts over Hiroshima and Nagasaki had made that claim come true. Faced with the prospect that any resumption of world-scale hostilities might literally wipe out life on Earth, the United Nations sought to establish an effective system of arms control. The West offered a form of international control of nuclear weapons in 1946-47 (the Baruch Plan), but this was rejected by the Soviet Union. Arkady Sobolev, the senior Russian official at the United Nations, explained that "the Soviet Union was not seeking equality, but, rather, freedom to pursue its own policies in complete freedom and without any interference or control from the outside." The USSR fielded a massive spy network in the West that climaxed with its own acquisition of a nuclear capability.

Ever since the NATO ministerial meetings in Bonn during the summer of 1957, arms control and mutual disarmament have been an essential component of the Alliance's strategy. The Western disarmament initiatives presented to the United Nations Disarmament Sub-Committee in August 1957 included: the reduction of all types of weapons and military forces; a decrease of existing stocks of nuclear weapons; suspension of nuclear testing; and adoption of protective measures against the risk of surprise attack. These recommendations were rejected by the Soviets and when the UN set up a Disarmament Commission to carry them through, nothing happened. As these and other efforts proved fruitless, peace, or at least the absence of war, came to rest on the fragile branch of the deterrence doctrine, with both sides in the East-West conflict building up their nuclear and conventional arsenals. The NATO doctrine eventually degenerated to a situation in which the Western Allies mortgaged their defence capability to a nuclear option, so that instead of genuine flexibility, any hostilities – even a strictly conventional attack – would trigger an escalation to nuclear retaliation. One of the earliest critics of this strategy was John Gellner, now editor of *The Canadian Defence Quarterly*, who testi-field before the House of Commons Special Committee on Defence in October 1963:

> In my opinion, nuclear weapons only deter nuclear war. They do not deter all kinds of war. I do not believe that the limitation of nuclear war is possible . . . and I do not believe that it can be "fought" in the sense that you conduct tactical operations in such a war.

The notion that a nuclear exchange would be nothing more than an ordinary war with magnified consequences may well be the most dangerous idea ever to be propagated. "Nuclear *war* is a term of deception," insists Dr. Bernard Lown, a leading member of the International Physicians for the Prevention of Nuclear War.

> War has been thought of as being an extension of politics, having defined objectives, with weapons of ascertainable destructiveness, with predictabilities as to outcome, with a possibility of defense measures to ameliorate casualties, with a role for medicine to care for the wounded, with winners and losers. But how is this relevant to an aftermath wherein blast, firestorm, and radioactive fallout destroy the very social fabric? What is the meaning of victory in the wake of a holocaust? It is essential to stop perceiving nuclear bombs as weapons, for they are not weapons but instruments of genocide. Nuclear war between the superpowers will be an unprecedented calamity, the most brutal verdict ever rendered against humankind.

Probably the most telling expression of the fear and loathing most people feel for the prospect of a nuclear exchange came from Nikita Khruschev, who prophesied that in any such war, "the living will envy the dead."

CANADA HAS ATTEMPTED, especially during Lester Pearson's time, to speak out for world disarmament. We have dedicated the efforts of many of our best ambassadors to these talks and formulations. But even if our voice is heard, it is seldom listened to: we possess little leverage in such sweepstakes, because we have so little to give up.

The United Nations, which should be the natural habitat for disarmament negotiations, has not had much better luck. The only disarmament document with any weight actually signed by members of the world body was the Limited Test Ban Treaty of 1963, renouncing above-ground nuclear tests. While this agreement did reduce radiation in the atmosphere, its chief effect was to drive nuclear testing underground. More tests have since been carried out under the earth's surface than were previously detonated in the sky. In 1980 alone, there were forty-nine, approximately four a month, including twenty by the Soviet Union, fourteen by the United States, eleven by France, three by the United Kingdom, and one by China. The Non-Proliferation Treaty adopted by the General Assembly of the United Nations in 1968 was meant to limit the acquisition of nuclear capability, but India and Israel have since added the weapons to their arsenals, and Pakistan, South Africa, Argentina, Brazil, and Iraq are close to making the required technological breakthroughs.

While nearly all the attention is focused on the Soviet Union and the United States, the march to nuclear armament is accelerating in other countries. The Swedish Institute of Peace Research estimates that in the 1980s at least two dozen nations will be able to make and launch atomic weapons. They include Italy, Japan, Switzerland, Taiwan, South Korea, Chile, Cuba, Iran, and Libya. Significantly, twelve countries which currently operate nuclear reactors have refused to sign the United Nations' Non-Proliferation Treaty. They are Cuba, Chile, South Africa, Pakistan, Vietnam, Israel, China, Spain, Argentina, France, Brazil, and India.

The American Office of Technology Assessment predicts it will soon be simple for a terrorist group to build small-yield nuclear weapons. "A terrorist group using stolen or diverted fission material, having technical competence but lacking direct weapon design experience, could probably build a weapon up to several kilotons," one of its studies concludes.

One specific incident illustrates that the counter-nuclear aspect of the arms race has already started. On June 7, 1981, Israel con-

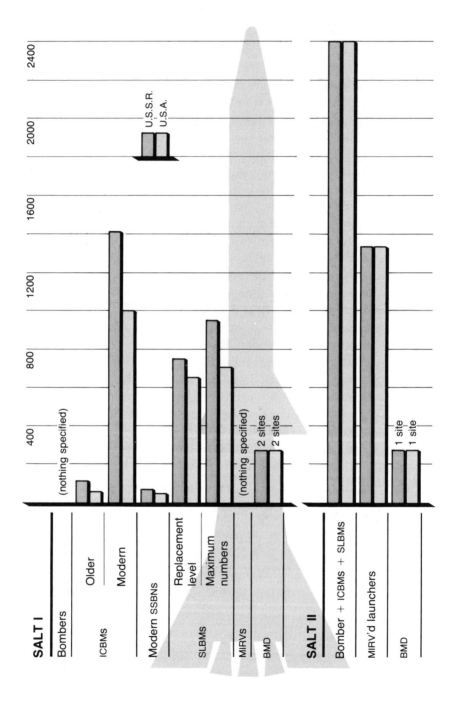

SALT I

Bombers — (nothing specified)

ICBMs
- Older
- Modern

Modern SSBNs

SLBMs
- Replacement level
- Maximum numbers

MIRVs — (nothing specified)

BMD
- 2 sites
- 2 sites

U.S.S.R.
U.S.A.

SALT II

Bomber + ICBMS + SLBMs

MIRV'd launchers

BMD
- 1 site
- 1 site

400   800   1200   1600   2000   2400

ducted the world's first pre-emptive strike against a nuclear facility by flying a thousand kilometers inside Iraq's territory and destroying its newly constructed Osiris-type reactor.

The highlight of nuclear disarmament negotiations between the superpowers was the Strategic Arms Limitation Treaty, signed in 1972 (SALT-I). It included a restrictive anti-ballistic-missile treaty and a so-called interim agreement temporarily freezing the level of American ICBMs at 1,054 – while allowing the USSR to increase their level up to 1,398. The Soviets were also permitted to maintain a superiority in submarine-launched ballistic missile (SLBM) launchers (950 versus 450), but comprehensive mutual restraint was never achieved. (The ABM treaty component was subject to review every five years; it was renewed in 1979 but has since not been seriously discussed. The SALT-II Treaty took seven years of negotiation, but it was never ratified by the U.S. Senate.) The limits specified by the anti-ballistic missile treaty and the interim agreement are shown in the chart on page 88.

Is there any realistic prospect of limiting the arms race?

The only hope is that the very nature of nuclear weapons could dictate the resumption of a dialogue that actually means something. "Before the advent of nuclear power, war, however devastating and brutal, had limits of destruction," Barbara Tuchman notes.

The Mongols may have left pyramids of skulls, and the Nazis the equivalent in their gas chambers, but their capacity was not global. Until now, the finality of the human race and its living space was not within the framework of expectation. Today it is, which gives the question of control an urgency it never had before.

Whatever military strategists may claim, there can be no real victor in a nuclear war; nuclear weapons are useful only as deterrents to war. Shortly before he was assassinated in 1979, Earl Mountbatten (whose distinguished public service career included six years as Britain's Chief of Defence Staff) declared that "the nuclear arms race has no military purpose. Wars cannot be fought with atomic weapons."

Despite Reagan's ambivalent stand on the issue, the most recent

Force Posture Statement to Congress by American Secretary of Defence Caspar W. Weinberger included this pledge:

> Today, deterrence remains – as it has for the past 37 years – the cornerstone of our strategic nuclear policy. To deter successfully, we must be able – and must be *seen* to be able – to respond to any potential aggression in such a manner that the costs we will exact will substantially exceed any gains the aggressor might hope to achieve. We, for our part, are under no illusions about the dangers of a nuclear war between the major powers; we believe that neither side could win such a war. But this recognition on our part is not sufficient to prevent the outbreak of nuclear war; it is essential that the Soviet leadership, in calculating the risks of aggression, recognizes that because of our retaliatory capability, there can be no circumstance in which it could benefit by beginning a nuclear war at any level or of any duration. If the Soviets recognize that our forces can and will deny them their objectives at whatever level of nuclear conflict they contemplate, and in addition that such a conflict could lead to the destruction of those political, military, and economic assets they value most highly, then deterrence is effective and the risk of war diminished.

CIVILIAN RESPONSE TO THE NUCLEAR THREAT has been particularly dramatic in Western Europe. The more than two million peace marchers who have shaken the NATO Alliance's solidarity were staging guerrilla theatre on a grand scale. It was a show of moral revulsion against the nuclear overkill certain to incinerate the continent in another war. Only the exclusion of the Soviet Union as a target for their anti-missile fury weakened the protesters' impact. The European Nuclear Disarmament (END) movement specifically left the Soviet Union out of its campaign by advocating a nuclear-free zone "from Poland to Portugal." When a Russian submarine carrying nuclear-tipped torpedoes rammed the Swedish mainland, there was no outcry from the peace marchers, and a protest rally in Stockholm drew only a puny group of four hundred.

Europe's peace movements are exercising their greatest influence by recruiting politicians in opposition parties who hold the balance of power in minority governments. These tactics have proved especially effective in Denmark, the Netherlands, and Belgium.

The Cold War warrior most openly contemptuous of the peace groups is Joseph Luns, the former Dutch foreign minister who has been Secretary-General of NATO since 1971. "It's all part of a relentless propaganda drive against America," he claims, "partly paid for and very much encouraged by the Soviet Union. There is more than enough circumstantial evidence that the KGB is financing much of the protest, and the Soviet ambassador to The Hague was decorated in the Kremlin for his efforts against the neutron bomb. Meanwhile, members of the peace movements in Norway, Denmark, and Sweden are strongly suspected of unwittingly receiving Soviet financial support."

Whether or not this is fact, it seems naïve to portray the United States and NATO as the roots of all evil in the arms race, with the benign Soviets reluctantly tagging along. Writing in the British weekly, *The Spectator*, Colin Welch noted:

It is hypocrisy which has abrogated to the Campaign for Nuclear Disarmament the beautiful word "peace," as though we do not all passionately desire peace, differing only about how best we think it can be preserved. It is hypocrisy which urges the "banning" of a bomb which nothing can now eradicate from human knowledge. It is hypocrisy which substitutes demonstrations and hysteria for rational argument about this complex and fateful issue. It is hypocrisy which points out (quite rightly) that nuclear deterrence is terribly dangerous and not wholly reliable, without suggesting any alternative. It is hypocrisy which equates Soviet communism and our imperfect western world, as though there were nothing to choose between them. It is hypocrisy which pretends to know what no one can know, that Russia has no designs on Western Europe. It is hypocrisy which continually refers to President Reagan as "bellicose" but never the late Brezhnev or the surviving Andropov, with his beguiling and deceitful proposals; which denounces the cruise missile as a "first-strike" weapon, when in fact it would take at least two hours to get to Moscow. Above all it is hypocritical to make no distinction between *possession* of the bomb and *use* of it.

THE ISSUE COMES DOWN to a conflict between societies based on differing value systems. Significantly, no disarmament movement has ever been allowed to flourish within the USSR. The wives of the men who organized the Group of Trust, the Soviet Union's first unofficial anti-war movement, told a Reuters correspondent in Moscow recently that they are convinced state authorities have decided to suppress the Group's activities completely. The nine women reported that after six months of harassment by the authorities, their husbands are facing criminal charges. Oleg Radzinsky, Alexander Shatravka, and Vladimir Mishchenko have already been arrested and are undergoing "psychiatric tests" in Moscow's Serbsky Institute before facing trial. "Our position is desperate and catastrophic," Natalya Batrovrina said, speaking for the Soviet Union's few declared pacifists.

In the United States elections on November 2, 1982, American voters in eight of the nine states where the issue was on the ballot endorsed, by overwhelming margins, a freeze on nuclear arms. The proposal for a mutual freeze – on the testing, production, and deployment of nuclear weapons and on missiles and new aircraft designed primarily to deliver nuclear weapons – as an essential, verifiable first step towards reducing the risk of nuclear war, was supported by 276 city councils. In addition, 446 New England town meetings, 56 county councils, and 11 state legislatures from Hawaii to New York voted to endorse such a freeze. More than 2.3 million Americans signed freeze petitions circulated by a host of organizations and coalitions. The cause inspired the largest demonstration in the country's history – the gathering on June 12, 1982, the occasion of the United Nations' second special session on disarmament, of nearly a million people in New York City.

During Canada's 1982 municipal elections, eighty cities in Ontario alone gave seventy-five per cent margins in favour of global disarmament. The issue has moved squarely into the mainstream of Canadian politics, with anti-nuclear war protestors crowding the downtowns of most Canadian cities. (Civil rights advocate Alan Borovoy once remarked that "in Canada we don't ban demonstrations, we reroute them.")

The essential element of any realistic disarmament policy is that it be mutual.

The singular failure by the world's political leaders to achieve any significant breakthroughs in forging realistic disarmament doctrines has given birth to the notion of deterrence. An enormous body of confusing literature has sprung up around this vague and difficult-to-define concept, but its central aim is simple: to influence the calculations of anyone who might consider aggression, and to influence them decisively and crucially before any attack is ever launched. Escalation is a matter of human decision, not an inexorable scientific process.

It is imperative to exploit whatever chance there might be of defusing escalated tensions short of a nuclear exchange. But that chance will always be precarious; amid the confusion, passions, and irrationalities of war, escalation always remains an inherent risk. The only safe course is prevention.

Planning deterrence means trying to think through an adversary's possible reasoning and contemplating in advance how alternative courses of action might appear to him. This must be done on his terms, allowing for the effects of future circumstances on his thinking. Neither side can be left with the agonizing dilemma of having no realistic alternative but surrender.

The world would be safer had nuclear weapons never been invented. But they can not be un-invented. The "balance" of power essential to the deterrence doctrine is a concept which has existed from earliest recorded history. A major cause of past wars has been a mismatch in the strength of actual or perceived military power.

The United States and the Soviet Union define the existing parameters of military deterrence. The present danger is that a nuclear conflict could come about as a result of processes beyond deterrence: sheer miscalculation, accident, or the result of a local quarrel.

At least for the foreseeable future, East-West relations will continue to be shaped by the irreducible dilemma of nuclear deterrence. As the stalemate in the competition for security and advantage persists, management of the nuclear arsenals will asume an increasingly ritualistic quality. Because the prospect of a radioactive holocaust is beyond imagination, future international behaviour may be insufficiently constrained to prevent smaller-scale conflicts.

Nuclear weapons have transformed the nature of war. Though they have been used only twice, half a lifetime ago, the scale of the horror at Hiroshima and Nagasaki makes it all the more essential that revulsion be partnered with clear thinking. It is necessary to render nuclear wars not just improbable, but impossible. But the abhorrence of war is no substitute for realistic plans to prevent its outbreak.

CHAPTER TEN

The Reluctant Virgin

*While we may not have our hand on the nuclear trigger,
our military commanders in Europe could well have their
thumbs on the microphone switches of the VHF radios that
request nuclear reinforcements for their threatened positions.*

T HE CANADIAN CONNECTION with nuclear weapons dates
back to the uranium we supplied for the original atomic
bombs dropped on Japan. On January 28, 1944, the federal government expropriated Gilbert LaBine's Eldorado mine at
Great Bear Lake. It was fissionable material from this source that
was used to build the bomb that exploded over Hiroshima on
August 6, 1945.*

Our more intimate involvement with nuclear weapons came
about as a result of some astonishingly naïve miscalculations by
John Diefenbaker during his term of office as Canada's thirteenth
prime minister. Though there was never a stated nuclear policy,
Diefenbaker ended up purchasing $685 million worth of weapons
for the Canadian armed forces which could only be utilized with
atomic warheads. Throughout the early 1960s, his government
continued to build up its arsenals of these weapons – while at the
same time loudly proclaiming its vaunted nuclear virginity.

The many advocates then urging Canada not to adopt nuclear
arms may have had a perfectly valid argument, but, by the fall of
1962, the choice was not – as Diefenbaker pretended it was –
between arming or not arming Canada's small but important
contribution to NATO and NORAD with atomic warheads. The only

---

*One-third of American nuclear weapons built from the late 1950s to the mid-1960s
used Canadian uranium.

remaining option was whether Canada should accept the American warheads or scrap $685 million worth of military hardware, thereby publicly reneging on international obligations voluntarily undertaken.

There was a time when more palatable alternatives had been available. The Diefenbaker government was not pushed into its nuclear predicament. Canada's acceptance of each of the four nuclear weapons systems involved an absurd sequence of events. In some ways, the choices made represented a characteristically Canadian but totally impractical compromise: we deliberately went out, purchased, and placed in the field, nuclear weapons systems – and then refused to accept the warheads that would make them an effective part of the Western deterrent.

In March 1960 the Canadian government decided to station a battery of Honest John rockets (a tactical artillery missile having a range of about twenty miles) with its Brigade Group in NATO. Our Honest John contingent was trained in Canada and dispatched to Europe in December 1961. Although non-nuclear Honest John warheads were said to exist, none were ordered – neither did the Diefenbaker government opt for any atomic warheads. Instead, the Honest Johns were stuffed with bags of sand.

The definition of a nuclear role for the Canadian Air Division in NATO followed a similar sequence. As the interceptor role for the Air Division's eight squadrons of F-86 day-fighters began to peter out in 1957, NATO military officials suggested that Canada might take on a strike-reconnaissance role, involving nuclear attack on military targets immediately behind the enemy's front line. The NATO planners picked this particular function for the Canadians because the RCAF contingent was the only one manned entirely by career airmen and was considered to be the best-trained among Allied formations. Also, unlike those of other groups, the planes could be converted to their new function without having to be taken out of service.

In May 1959, General Lauris Norstad, the Supreme Allied Commander of NATO, went to Ottawa to brief the Diefenbaker Cabinet on exactly what the strike-reconnaissance role entailed. Canadian military men were skeptical about whether the ministry would agree to the proposal, because it involved a fundamental shift in the nature of the Canadian commitment: instead of remaining entirely a defensive force, the Canadian contingent in NATO would be expected to fly offensive strikes against specified targets in East Germany and other East European countries. But the Conservative administration accepted the assignment and pledged to have eight squadrons of the new aircraft operational by May 1, 1963. Barely two months later, the Canadian government reaffirmed its intention to fulfill the promise made to Norstad. The Lockheed Starfighter (CF-104) was selected for the NATO Air Division as a replacement for the F-86, and a contract for $431 million was negotiated with Canadair Limited in Montreal to manufacture two hundred of the aircraft.

The first full squadron of CF-104s was formed at the RCAF base in Zweibrücken, West Germany, in December 1962, five months earlier than Diefenbaker had pledged that our new NATO contribution would be operational. But in order to meet the May 1, 1963, deadline, the Canadian government would have had to have signed a nuclear agreement with the United States on or before November 1, 1962.

This would have involved two contracts: a general government-to-government agreement and a series of technical negotiations between the defence departments of the two countries, covering custodial, security, and training arrangements for the weapons. Neither was settled as long as Diefenbaker remained prime minister – and so the CF-104 took its place beside the Honest John as yet another totally useless weapon.

The more complicated chain of events that eventually led to the acquisition of nuclear equipment (if not warheads) for the domestic defence of Canada, began on July 27, 1957, when John Foster Dulles went to Ottawa for his first official call on the recently elected Conservative administration. Five days later Defence Minister George Pearkes announced that Canada and the United States had agreed to establish integrated control for the air defence of their countries in a new organization to be known as the North American Air Defence Command, with headquarters at Colorado Springs, Colorado. Air Marshal Roy Slemon, then the RCAF's Chief of Staff, was named Deputy Commander-in-Chief of the new organization, which became operational on September 12.

It then appeared that Canada's main contribution to continental air defence would be the CF-105 Arrow all-weather, supersonic interceptor, being built at the Malton, Ontario, plant of A. V. Roe Canada Limited. The initial 1953 contract had envisaged an eventual production of five hundred aircraft at an estimated unit cost of $2 million. By 1958, the contract had been set at thirty-seven pre-production models with orders for an eventual one hundred planes. Development costs had by this time exceeded $300 million, and the per-plane cost by the time the first Arrow flew on March 25, 1958, was running close to $7 million.

On September 23, 1958, Diefenbaker announced that the entire Arrow program would be subject to review in six months. On February 20, 1959, six weeks ahead of his own deadline, Diefenbaker told a hushed House of Commons that the Arrow contract was being terminated immediately. The five existing Arrows were sold to Waxman's junk yard in Hamilton, Ontario, and callously destroyed. The death of the plane, which symbolized the future of Canada's aviation industry, represented a choice by the government as fundamental as the decision a decade earlier by the Royal Navy to scrap its capital ships. The government was committing itself to the notion that enemy bombers should be intercepted by missiles, not planes.

In place of the Arrow, Diefenbaker announced that Canada planned to acquire two squadrons of Bomarc "B" anti-aircraft missiles for installation at North Bay, Ontario, and La Macaza, Quebec. The United States was at that time planning to erect thirty Bomarc bases along its northern approaches. Since this meant that, in case of attack, a major atomic air battle would take place directly over Toronto and Montreal, the Diefenbaker government had persuaded the Pentagon to move two of the bases, originally scheduled to be built in northern Michigan and northern New York state, into Canada, to be sited north of our metropolitan centres. The Americans agreed to pay for the missiles, thus reducing the Canadian share of the Bomarc program to less than $14 million.

In announcing the switch to the Bomarc, Diefenbaker did not specify that the new weapons would carry nuclear warheads. However, the implications of such a policy were there because no conventional warhead for the Bomarc "B" Model had ever been designed or manufactured. (In the development stages of the Bomarc "A" Model, a high-explosive warhead had been used, but it was scrapped for the miniaturized nuclear version.)

The prime minister further strengthened his own pro-nuclear case in his February 20 House of Commons announcement which stressed that, since "the full potential of these defensive weapons is achieved only when they are armed with nuclear warheads," negotiations had started with the United States for the acquisition of atomic armaments. On May 25, 1959, an agreement between the two countries was tabled outlining an "exchange of nuclear information for mutual defence." It covered the training of Canadian troops in the use of nuclear weapons, but included no mention of any Canadian obligation to actually accept them.

The Diefenbaker government never did acquire the warheads. During the negotiations for the Bomarc and the Voodoo, Canadian cabinet ministers had assured their United States opposite numbers that they *would* arm the weapons in an emergency, but didn't want to upset the domestic political situation by publicizing a nuclear commitment.

When the time came for the Conservative cabinet to approve acceptance of the warheads, another issue arose. The Americans insisted that, under Section 92 of the United States Atomic Energy Act, American atomic warheads could not be transferred out of their custody. They would, therefore, have to send special troops into Canada to guard them. This fact, though it had been made obvious when the weapons were first purchased, appalled Diefenbaker's more nationalistic ministers. They persuaded their colleagues not to allow these Yankee soldiers into the country: it had taken two world wars to get Canada's armed forces away from British control, and now they would be subjected to "foreign orders" once again.

While Diefenbaker found it politically useful to exploit the notion of American dominance, he and his ministers were well aware of the legislative limitations of American nuclear policies and the resultant "two-key" system of control which required the decision of both governments to release the warheads. His posturing was oriented for domestic political consumption, since he had already agreed, at the North Atlantic Council meetings in December 1957, to the position from which he was now trying to back away. It was and it has always been extremely delicate and difficult (if not impossible) to establish any position which separates Canada philosophically or even politically from any part of NATO's strategy. As early as the mid-1950s, Canada participated in developing the tactical doctrine and organizational framework for operations on the nuclear battlefield. Canadian soldiers, sailors, and airmen witnessed the explosion of tactical nuclear devices in the summer of 1957 at Desert Rock in Nevada.

At any rate, by February 1, 1982, the RCAF had taken over the completed Bomarc base in North Bay – but since the Diefenbaker government refused to accept the nuclear warheads, and since no conventional alternatives existed, the Bomarcs remained headless, rusting in their cradles.

United States military strategists were understandably upset by the Canadian government's attitude. They had moved the two bases north of their border – and outside their control – at Canada's insistence. Under Diefenbaker's non-nuclear policy, the main corridor of potential Russian attack into the industrial heartland of the eastern United States now lacked whatever protection was afforded by the Bomarcs. Although the American Bomarc program had been cut to only eight bases, the missile was still considered an effective weapon against bombers – but only if armed with nuclear warheads.

One argument the Americans used to urge Canadian adoption of the atomic charges was that this would actually *reduce* the amount of radioactivity spilled on Canada in any future war. According to this dubious theory, the successful interception of Soviet bombers bound for North American targets was most likely to occur over Canada. The Soviets would almost certainly arm their planes with "dead-man fuses" – gadgets that automatically detonate their atomic bombs at pre-set altitudes whether or not the bombers' flight crew is still alive. A Russian attack intercepted by Bomarcs armed only with high explosives would rain the fused nuclear weapons from the bomb bays of the downed enemy aircraft onto Canada, spreading clouds of fallout as they burst. But Bomarcs carrying atomic warheads would be able to "cook" the incoming bombers and their nuclear loads without setting off the bombs. Instead of the massive devastation caused by the fused bombs, the territory below the air battle would be subjected only to relatively minor nuclear explosions.

The same argument was used by Pentagon officials to urge nuclear warheads for the CF-101B Voodoo jet interceptors. The Diefenbaker government had ordered the Voodoos from the United States in a swap deal involving the manning by Canada of sixteen radar stations on the Pinetree Line. The decision to obtain sixty-four of the American fighters for the RCAF Air Defence Command was announced on June 12, 1961. The planes originally came into service in the spring of 1962, armed with conventional Falcon rockets instead of the nuclear-tipped Genie missiles carried by Voodoos in the USAF.

What really puzzled the American defence officials, whose hemispheric responsibility included Canada, was Diefenbaker's apparent misunderstanding of the deterrence concept on which the world's uneasy nuclear balance was based. Late in 1961, the Canadian prime minister began to hint that he had solved his nuclear dilemma: the warheads would be brought into the country (and presumably accepted by our NATO contingents in Europe) just *before* the outbreak of any future nuclear war.

Aside from the American claim that modern warfare simply does not allow time for such a pre-hostilities trucking rodeo, Washington officials insisted that the Canadian attitude undermined the very basis of deterrence which depends on fully-armed, ready-to-shoot weapons being in place to discourage the enemy from ever starting his attack.

When General Norstad, who could speak out because two days earlier he had retired from his post as Supreme Commander of the NATO forces, returned to Ottawa on January 3, 1962, he held a press conference at which he openly attacked the Canadian government for not living up to its commitments. Told of Norstad's statement, General Charles Foulkes, the former Chairman of the Canadian Chiefs of Staff then living in retirement near Victoria, British Columbia, confirmed its accuracy. "There was a definite commitment, and there is no excuse that Canada didn't know what it was letting itself into," he said. "It is unfair to give our military forces tasks and then leave them unable to carry them out. It is also not part of the Canadian character to renege on an agreement."

Conservative spokesmen belittled the Norstad revelations by pointing out that, as a retired general, he had "no more official standing than any other American tourist," but the issue eventually split the Conservative cabinet, prompting the resignation of Minister of Defence Douglas Harkness.

The issue had come to symbolize Diefenbaker's mood of indecision. This hesitation was not politically significant until the Liberal leader, Lester Pearson (prompted by a confidential memorandum from Paul Hellyer), gave a speech on January 23, 1963, reversing his party's position and calling for the acceptance of the warheads. This dramatic switch, enhanced by Diefenbaker's continued inability to articulate any defence policy of his own, led to the breakup three weeks later of the Conservative Cabinet and to the party's defeat in the Commons. The Liberals won the election that followed with a minority mandate and armed all the controversial weapons systems with nuclear tips. The Bomarcs were declared operational on January 16, 1964, and stayed in service until they were declared obsolete and dismantled eight years later. Similarly, the nuclear elements of Canada's NATO contingent were placed in active service until, in September 1970, Pierre Trudeau, who had succeeded Pearson as Liberal leader in 1968, reduced Canada's NATO commitments.

Although the political record seems to indicate that we stumbled into adopting a nuclear strategy during the Diefenbaker years, our official, accredited representatives participated actively in the evolution of every NATO strategy, including its nuclear components. This dates back to the Harmel Report and development of the original NATO Nuclear Planning Group, of which Canada was a charter member. At no time has Canada officially denied the need for NATO to possess a credible deterrent based on tactical, intermediate, and strategic nuclear weapons. At the moment, our mini-brigade groups are committed in operational areas where, in the face of enemy incursions, the need to call for nuclear fire support could develop. While we may not have our hand on the nuclear trigger, our military commanders in Europe could well have their thumbs on the microphone switches of the VHF radios that request nuclear reinforcements for their threatened positions.

And yet, because of the actual weapons we now possess, we are about to decamp from that self-selected club of nations which possess nuclear military capabilities.

Four Canadian bases are currently geared to receive nuclear warheads. They are located at Comox, British Columbia, North Bay, Ontario, Bagotville, Quebec, and Chatham, New Brunswick. Custody is maintained exclusively by the United States Air Force, but the Genie warheads are ready to be released for use by Canadian aircraft in the event of an emergency.

The Genies are the only nuclear weapon remaining in Canada's arsenal. They are mounted on the wings of the CF-101s that form part of the NORAD screen. The fifty-five Voodoos involved, now more than twenty years old, are due to be scrapped and replaced by the new CF-18s. These new aircraft will *not* be armed with nuclear-tipped missiles but will instead use the conventional Sidewinders and Sparrows.

This will remove the last nuclear warheads in Canadian custody. We will have become nuclear virgins at last.

CHAPTER ELEVEN

Bruise for a Cruise

*Few of the technicalities about the cruise are understood
by the general public. But Canadians have a way of smelling a rat.*

T HE RACE BETWEEN THE SUPERPOWERS to build up their
bristles of primed missiles dates back to the Cuban Crisis
of 1962 when the gap between them became most obvious.
At the time, the USSR had sixty-four operational long-range missiles (most of which required a ten-hour fuelling-up period) while
the Americans possessed a ready arsenal of sixteen hundred
modern projectiles.

The calculus of these deadly missiles has since become the substance of intensive international debate, with the propaganda
apparatus of both the Kremlin and the Pentagon pumping out
their own weighted statistics. *The Economist*, in its *Foreign
Report*, published on February 24, 1983, attempted to place the
totals in an objective perspective, and came up with the following
comparison:

	USA	USSR
Intercontinental ballistic missiles	1,046	1,398
Submarine-launched ballistic missiles	544	950
	1,590	2,348

During the late 1970s the Russians had begun to deploy a new
generation of medium-range ballistic missiles (the SS-20s) on their
western borders. The members of NATO (Canada included) delib-
erated on the significance of this disruption of what was previously a parity of strategic nuclear weapons. The unanimous conclu-

sion was that the numbers of the new missiles, their mobility, possession of triple warheads, re-load capability, and the fact that they were facing no effective European-based deterrent, had profoundly altered the NATO/Warsaw Pact balance of power. The theory was that without any new and visibly powerful deterrent based on the continent, the SS-20s would have precisely the effect long sought by the Soviet Union: the separation of the United States from its European NATO partners, leading inevitably to the "Finlandization" of the continent. It was to even out the credibility of their deterrent that NATO, prompted by Helmut Schmidt of West Germany, asked the United States to deploy more nuclear weapons in Western Europe.

In December 1979, the NATO partners unanimously agreed that 572 new missiles would be installed by 1984. The 108 Pershing II intermediate-range ballistic missiles were all to be deployed in West Germany, but would remain under American control, while 464 ground-launched cruise missiles were to be installed on mobile ground launchers in five countries: 96 on twenty-four launchers in West Germany; 160 on forty launchers in Britain; 112 on twenty-eight launchers in Italy; 48 on twelve launchers in Belgium; and 48 on twelve launchers in the Netherlands. NATO tried to accommodate West Germany's insistence that it would not accept modernized missiles unless at least one NATO member other than Britain (which has its own nuclear weapons) did so. Otherwise, West Germany claimed, as the sole provider of bases for American medium-range missiles that could, for the first time, reach Soviet territory, it would feel too exposed to Soviet propaganda initiatives. Thus, acceptance of the missiles by Belgium, the Netherlands, and Italy became supremely important.

Opposition to these new weapons in Europe has created a crisis. Underneath the diplomatic rhetoric of Alliance solidarity, NATO is sharply divided, with those members which favour the cruise deployment – United States and Britain – showing increasing impatience with those who oppose it – mainly the Scandilux group of nations.

THE CRUISE IS CONTROVERSIAL because it is a qualitatively different kind of weapon. "Cruise," strictly speaking, is an adjective, not a noun, so that to discuss "the Cruise" is as meaningless as to talk about "the Ballistic." "Cruise" describes the missile's locomotion through space: it lifts with wings like an airplane, as opposed to the trajectory of ballistic flight which more closely resembles the curve of a ball thrown to a catcher over the horizon.

Essentially an unmanned airplane, the cruise is hardly a new weapon. Nazi Germany built and fired many V-1 flying bombs during the Second World War, as well as V-2s, which were early ballistic missiles. Both superpowers have developed several cruise models, although up to now the Soviet versions are larger and more cumbersome than the American. Recent developments in microelectronics have allowed American engineers to pack the advanced guidance system (the LN-35, made by Litton Systems Canada Ltd.) into a small space, while compact jet engines give the weapon its long range.

As the table on page 108 (adapted from *U.S. Cruise Missile Programs* by Charles A. Sorrels, McGraw-Hill, 1983) clearly illustrates, these are separate, quite different weapons, though they share the Tercom (terrain contour matching) guidance system that makes them accurate enough to be aimed between the goal posts of a football field up to 1,550 miles away. The funds being allocated to the cruise ($25.2 billion plus $3.3 billion for research) mark this as one of the Pentagon's major new weapons systems. The fact that nearly twelve thousand of the missiles are on order — each due to be armed with a nuclear warhead with a potency of up to 200 kilotons — documents their deadly nature.

Because of their relatively low unit costs, their versatility, and their ability to be used with existing ships and aircraft, the cruise missile system is much favoured by American military planners.

The Soviet Union has equipped its forces with cruise missiles for more than a decade. In fact, it was a Soviet anti-ship cruise missile (classified as the SSN2-Styx) fired by the Egyptians which sank the Israeli destroyer *Elath* during the 1967 war. The large, nuclear-powered, Russian Oscar-class submarines carry twenty-four anti-ship cruise missiles, as do the Kirov-class cruisers.

Dangerous as it undoubtedly is, the cruise is *not*, as many of its opponents claim, a first-strike weapon. A first-strike weapon is

There are four basic CRUISE systems currently being developed in the U.S.

Type	Size	Weight	Development commenced	Planned installation	Number	Cost ($ millions)	Launch platforms
SLCM Sea-Launched Cruise Missile	Width 2.6 m, Length 5.5 m	1200 kg	1972	Mid 1984	3,994	$10,348.	Nuclear submarines
ALCM Air-Launched Cruise Missile	Width 3.6 m, Length 6.2 m	1350 kg	1974	1982	4,348	$ 6,922.	B52G, B52H and B1B bombers
GLCM Ground-Launched Cruise Missile	Width 2.6 m, Length 5.5 m	1200 kg	1977	Dec. 1983	560	$ 2,945.	Ground mobile launchers
MRASM Medium-Range Air-to-Surface Cruise Missile	Width 2.6 m, Length 5.9 m	1450 kg	1980	1986	2,500	$ 5,000.	B52G bombers F16 fighters

defined as a strategic ballistic missile that can be launched without warning and can reach its target so swiftly that it inflicts major damage before the enemy can react. The maximum range of a cruise missile is about fifteen hundred miles. Its maximum speed of five hundred miles per hour makes it slower than some commercial jets, and much slower than most fighters and bombers. Since the Soviet Union already possesses the technology to shoot down such jets, the cruise hardly ranks as first-strike. (If one of the European-based cruise missiles were to be fired near Frankfurt, it would take two and a half hours to reach Moscow. If one of the Soviet triple-warhead SS-20 missiles based near Moscow were to be fired at Frankfurt, it would get there in eight minutes.)

Nearly all the controversy about the new NATO nuclear deployments has been concerned with the cruise. But the Pershing II, which will be installed early in 1984, will be an even more awesomely de-stabilizing weapon. Its speed and accuracy are such that, launched from their bases near Frankfurt, for example, the Pershing II will be able to hit a guard pacing in front of Lenin's tomb at the Kremlin, precisely *six minutes* later. "When the Pershing II is deployed," warns Arthur Macy Cox, author of *Russian Roulette: the Superpower Game*,

> we will have forced the Russians into a corner. They will almost certainly adopt a policy of launch on warning, which means that they launch missiles on first warning of attack rather than risk having their command centres destroyed. Since no human decision-making system can be responsive in six minutes, the Russians will have to rely on computers. Their computers are not as advanced as ours, and ours make errors.

ONE FACTOR THAT will increase the hazards of installing the cruise missile is that, except for the deployment of the ground-based European version, it has been designed as a "usable" weapon — one that is seen not as a deterrent but as an integral part of nuclear war-fighting strategy. Because the cruise has been proven to be vulnerable to the more sophisticated advances in Soviet radar technology, the United States has decided to make it one of the first weapons clothed in "stealth" (radar-deceiving) technology.

It is difficult to have preferences among nuclear weapons. They all herald the end of civilization, and there is little point in believing that one type of missile is better or worse than any other. What makes the cruise so different — and ultimately so dangerous — is that it is the first of the atomic delivery systems which is unverifiable. This is not due to its relatively small size or the versatility of its launching methods. The problem is that any *limitations* placed on the use and armaments of the cruise are impossible to verify. The SALT-II talks, for example, specifically applied to cruise missiles with ranges of more than six hundred miles, but the actual range of the missile is impossible to detect because it is so simple to vary the amount of fuel and nuclear explosives inside each identical casing. For the same reason, it is impossible for outside observers to verify whether a cruise is armed with conventional or nuclear warheads. Arms control depends on monitored compliance of the agreed-to limits. Introduction of the cruise threatens to upset this precarious balance.

FEW OF THE TECHNICALITIES about the cruise are understood by the general public. But Canadians have a way of smelling a rat.

The Canadian public, after apparently sleeping through two decades of having nuclear-weapons-carrying aircraft (the Genie used by our NORAD fighters) on its soil, has suddenly woken up and decided to oppose the testing of the American cruise missile — even though they have been assured that no warheads, conventional or nuclear, are to be used.

From the beginning, the Trudeau government has maintained that this particular test of this specific missile over that special stretch of northern Alberta was required to meet our commitments to NATO, and that its overflights could be used as a bargaining lever in prompting the Soviets to take disarmament more seriously.

Neither of these arguments is true.

This is *not* the weapon that will be deployed in Europe (that will be a ground, not air, launched weapon); the territory which the NATO cruise missiles will traverse in their flight to predetermined

110

Soviet targets will be over industrialized eastern Europe and not over land comparable to northern Alberta. These cruise missiles have no connection with the weapons under discussion at the Geneva disarmament talks. The missile we have agreed to test is a second-generation, *strategic* weapon, which will be launched by United States Strategic Air Command bombers directly across the North Pole at Russian cities. They will be under American, not NATO command, and will belong to the U.S. retaliatory arsenal, rather than being part of any alliance to which we belong.

As Richard Gwyn reported in the *Toronto Star*, these cruise missiles have not only already been tested, but are classified as operational by the United States Air Force: "The manufacturer, Boeing Aircraft Corp., has already bragged about it. According to one of its ads, it has been building Air-Launched Cruise missiles at the rate of 40 per month since October, 1982. These reached 'initial operational capability' last December, and have passed 'every test with flying colours, including a thumbs-up flight test program.'"

The Second World War battleships reactivated by President Reagan are being equipped with thirty-two cruise missiles each, and many successful tests of this weapon (called the Tomahawk) have already been flown from the USS *New Jersey*. According to a recent issue of the authoritative *Aviation Week & Space Technology*, 103 tests had been completed by June 1983. (The magazine story cited 75 of the tests as having been successful.) Testing the unarmed vehicles over Canada is required only to fine tune their guidance system. Refusing the United States permission to test will not make an iota of practical difference to the deployment and manufacture of the cruise; what it will do is put a serious dent in North American solidarity and make disarmament negotiations that much more difficult.

The British magazine *The Spectator* recently noted:

The deployment of cruise missiles in Britain and other parts of Western Europe has become a matter of confidence. It is important not so much because of what the missiles can actually do, but as a symbol of the Alliance's defensive determination. Given the opposition from Russia and the indigenous Left, their deployment has now become necessary, almost regardless of the missile's usefulness. The Russians will not bother to negotiate seriously on arms reduction with opponents who are reducing their own arms anyway.

That may be a valid reason for deploying the cruise in Europe. It has nothing to do with testing the weapons in Canada.

Historically, there is no inherent reason why we should refuse to test our Allies' weapons. It is a long-established tradition among NATO allies to test one another's weapons. As Ron Lowman, the military analyst for the *Toronto Star*, has pointed out, the results of highly secret tests against chemical and biological weapons carried out by the Defence Research Establishment near Suffield, Alberta, have been shared by an international agreement first signed in 1942 by the United States, Britain, and Australia. "Back in the 1960s, during the Vietnam War," Lowman reported,

> sections of Canadian Forces Base Gagetown were sprayed from a U.S. helicopter with defoliating chemicals, ostensibly at the request of the Canadian Forces. The army was said to be bothered by grass and timber re-growth. A Pentagon spokesman in Washington has confirmed that the tests were made because some trees in New Brunswick were similar to trees in Viet Nam, which the U.S. wanted to defoliate so that enemy forces couldn't use them for cover. A multi-million dollar lawsuit has been launched in the U.S. by veterans who claim to have been contaminated by the defoliant Agent Orange. U.S. lawyer Victor Yannacone says that until 1968, two years after the Gagetown spraying, Agent Orange was laced with the deadly chemical dioxin.

Other manoeuvres regularly carried out on Canadian soil include tank and infantry exercises by British and West German troops at Suffield, Alberta, and Shilo, Manitoba; ultra-low flying operations by the American Air Force out of Goose Bay, Labrador; and use of our Nanoose torpedo range off the West Coast by the American Navy. "Perhaps the best training of the year for fighter pilots of the Canadian Forces, the RAF, the USAF, the US Navy and the US Marine Corps," wrote Lowman, "are the May-and-September Exercise Maple Flag at Cold Lake, Alberta. They can dogfight with expert monitoring from a computer known as the Air Combat Manoeuvring Range, and attack ground targets with live ammunition, bombs and rockets."

BUT THE CRUISE IS DIFFERENT. Its proposed overflights have roused deeply-felt indignation, even among Canadians who haven't given the country's defence matters a second thought for a generation.

Such widespread furor cannot either be succumbed to – as a line of least political resistance – or dismissed by the simplistic statement that we have to test the cruise missile just because we're partners in NATO.

West German Defence Minister Manfred Woerner has confirmed that the cruise to be tested in Canada is not part of the weapons system being deployed in Western Europe.

Trudeau's argument that we must proceed with the tests or leave NATO is a blatant untruth. Norway refused to test the cruise; Denmark and Holland have unofficially notified the Alliance that they will not consent to having the weapons installed on their soil; Iceland has no weapons of any kind – yet all of these countries are considered to be members in good standing of NATO. "The real reason for Ottawa's decision on the cruise," wrote historian Desmond Morton in the *Toronto Star*, "is that it is a cheap counter to the Canada-bashers who cluster in Washington these days. With memories of Ken Taylor and the Teheran Caper long since vanished, testing the cruise is a trade-off for action on acid rain, gas sales, freeing the kidnapped Sid Jaffe and a host of other, cross-border irritants."

Professor Morton is right, but he doesn't go far enough. The Trudeau government also considers the cruise as a trade-off in another direction: by agreeing to test the weapon, the Trudeau administration is convinced it can get the NATO Allies, now pressuring Canada to spend some real money on *conventional* defence, off its back. The tests, the Liberals hope, will take the place of some of the meaningful steps essential to strengthening our defence potential.

Still, with the cruise controversy having been blown up to its current proportions, Canada cannot ethically refuse the tests without proposing some equally significant compensating act. What is required is a clear, unequivocal declaration that Canada does not intend to test the cruise, but that instead – to demonstrate our continuing loyalty to the notion of multilateral defence – we intend to double our expenditures on *conventional* weapons in the next five years. In return for that firm undertaking, we would expect NATO to relieve us of whatever commitments exist to test the cruise.

Dramatic as it sounds, such a leap in defence spending would take us only to the same level (just over three per cent of GNP) as most of the other NATO nations.

By offering this proposal Ottawa would be giving NATO (which has been strenuously advocating an increased defence effort by Canada) and the anti-cruise demonstrators a course of action that would satisfy the demands of both.

CHAPTER TWELVE

Threats and Counter-threats

"Not even the most passionate ideologue will be able to tell the ashes of Capitalism from those of Communism – for, among other reasons, he too will be dead."
JOHN KENNETH GALBRAITH

ONE OF THE PROBLEMS OF TRYING to bring reason to bear on future Canadian defence policy is that so much of the military planning by both superpowers involves interplanetary ideas that make the wars fought in the old Buck Rogers comics seem like schoolyard mud-slinging romps. The time element involved in the missile exchanges contemplated by East-West strategists for the destruction of each others' intercontinental ballistic missile arsenals is a good example. Here the observer enters a bizarre world in which time and space are measured in split-second pulses that mean the survival of one nation and the destruction of another.* If an intercontinental ballistic missile of the type now mounted in underground silos both in the United States and in the Union of Soviet Socialist Republics, was fired from southwestern Russia at, say, Toronto, it would hit there about thirty minutes later.

If Toronto were by then protected by anti-ballistic missiles, the incoming missile would presumably be intercepted and "cooked" (i.e., destroyed without a nuclear explosion) somewhere high over the North Pole. But the problems involved in locating and destroying such a weapon are prohibitively intricate. The exact size of the

---

*President Reagan recently commented favourably on the skills American teenagers were developing by playing electronic games, and suggested that they might be the fighter pilots of the future. It's chilling to realize that as these young people reach adulthood, a new generation of electronic weapons will have been developed on which they will be able to try out their skills for real.

warheads on Soviet missiles isn't known, but American intelligence experts estimate that the largest of them isn't much bigger than an office desk. That's the dimension of the projectile – rushing out of space towards its target at a speed of at least twenty thousand miles an hour. The counter-missile must destroy it. To be of any use, any defensive system must stop *all* – not just most – incoming weapons. It must also be able to distinguish among decoys, meteorites, space junk, and the real thing – all within the first five minutes of the missile's parabolic descent.

To get around this problem, one group of American researchers recently broached the possibility of basing nuclear missiles on the moon – the idea being that they'd be safe from surprise attack there because any weapon launched from Earth would take about forty-eight hours to reach the lunar installation. This would theoretically give the moon-based operators plenty of time to respond with missiles of their own.

That's only a mildly looney idea compared with the suggestion once made to the American Astronautical Society by Dandridge Cole of General Electric's space vehicle department. His plan was to explode a cluster of hydrogen bombs behind one of the asteroids orbiting between the Earth and Mars, then to guide this "lost planet" into the Soviet subcontinent. It would hit with the force of several million H-bombs. According to this preposterous theory, the few stunned Siberians who might survive, thinking it had all been a natural catastrophe, wouldn't release any retaliatory bombs of their own.

If this sounds improbable, think about the armed satellites soon to be orbiting above us. A satellite 22,300 miles up travels at the same speed as the Earth spins on its axis. That means that the satellite remains suspended over any fixed position on the Earth's surface. It's hypothetically feasible to have, say, two dozen H-bombs, mounted on satellites, hovering permanently over any enemy's twenty-four main population centres – to be set off at a split-second's notice.

Another new threat (already with us, though its full potential has yet to be appreciated by either side) is what's called the "electromagnetic pulse" syndrome (EMP). This phenomenon occurs when there is a nuclear explosion at high altitudes. The gamma rays released encounter electrons at the upper atmosphere, and the electrons are accelerated by the gamma ray collisions. When they reach the earth's magnetic field, electrons generate enormous electrical currents with peak strength of fifty thousand volts per metre. The effect extends over thousands of kilometres. A single nuclear blast high above the United States or the USSR could shut down the power grid and knock out the entire communication system of either country. A ten-megaton burst at an altitude of four hundred kilometres would destroy electrical equipment from coast to coast. Given any serious international crisis, the EMP syndrome would tempt one side or the other toward a policy of pre-emption – launching one's missiles before detonation of the first attacking weapon – while electrical and communications networks are still intact.

Quite apart from these promised horrors of modern science, a whole generation of "psychochemical" weapons is now being "think-tanked." Instead of attacking an enemy's cities, they would destroy his will to fight. Preliminary experiments with animals have already established the potency of these new agents by, quite literally, making cats flee in terror from mice.

Perhaps the most frightening prospect of all is the full militarization of space. This scenario envisages nuclear-torpedo-equipped space craft and orbital laser battle platforms circling the earth as they stalk enemy targets below. According to Professor Stephen M. Meyer of the Center for International Studies at the Massachusetts Institute of Technology, several production programs (in both the United States and the Soviet Union) are currently directed toward the development of precisely such space-weapons systems.

In the summer of 1982, the *Los Angeles Times* reported the test flight of the world's first fighter space craft, an unmanned, twenty-ton vehicle launched by the USSR from a site near the Caspian Sea and dropped by parachute into the Pacific, where a seven-ship USSR fleet was waiting to pick it up. The Soviets also have in their possession an anti-satellite killer known as Cosmos 1379, which has been successfully tested.

It would be reassuring to be able to laugh off all this as nothing more than *Star Wars* fantasy, but it's only too real. In a series of press conferences during the last week of March 1983, President Ronald Reagan called for the United States to develop orbiting anti-satellite systems to counter similar moves by the Soviets. The USSR is known to be building hunter-killer space craft equipped with laser beams that would disable space craft orbiting close to Earth. Not much data is available about other Russian efforts, except that they are centred in the Baikonur Cosmodrome in Central Asia. The United States plans to have two satellite attack squadrons operational by 1985, flying out of Langley Air Force Base in Virginia. At the same time, American intelligence sources indicate that the Soviets are developing an underground nuclear test centre at Semipalatinsk, northeast of Tashkent, and a new type of charge-particle beam at Saryshagan. They claim that these rays could destroy American ballistic missiles before they disperse their warheads – granting the Soviets a distinct advantage over the United States.

Unlike the American MX system, the Soviet SS-18 and SS-19 ICBMs are already in place. During the past decade, the Soviets have developed four new long-range missile systems. This has been the rationale for President Reagan's push to build the MX missiles, which will carry ten warheads each, capable of being independently targeted on objectives as small as a henhouse at the other end of the Earth.

THE MX AFFAIR BROUGHT INTO THE OPEN the altered focus of American defence strategy. Even though the world has lived with the atomic bomb for two generations, the idea of an actual nuclear war between the superpowers still defies comprehension. Jonathan Schell in *The Fate of the Earth* makes it clear that there are now more than enough nuclear warheads for the superpowers to annihilate each other and, effectively, life on Earth as well, and that "winning" a nuclear war is a delusion. "It has sometimes been claimed that the United States could survive a nuclear attack by the Soviet Union, but the bare figures on the extent of the blast waves, the thermal pulses, and the accumulated local fallout dash this hope irrevocably. They spell the doom of the United States. And if one imagines the reverse attack on the Soviet Union, its doom is spelled out in similar figures." Canada will not be spared the same doom.

Whether a nuclear exhange would end in a global holocaust or in a relatively limited exchange of weapons that would leave at least some human life on Earth, no one can be absolutely sure, but out of such calculations has come the theory of limited war: that the only credible deterrent to a nuclear battle is the willingness to fight one. American Vice-President George Bush has spoken of "an emerging winner" in a nuclear exchange. But most defence critics believe that the mere discussion of "winnable" nuclear war increases the chance of one occurring.

This notion of a "survivable nuclear war" marks the end of a long evolution in American strategic thinking. Under President Eisenhower, U.S. nuclear doctrine was based on the threat of "massive retaliation" to punish Russian adventurism in areas deemed vital to the West. When Sputnik's flight demonstrated Soviet technological ability to deliver warheads over long distances, this strategy turned to deterrence. At that point, the only imaginable outcome of a nuclear exchange was reciprocal devastation. Simply *having* nuclear weapons became a deterrent to their use. This strategy was aptly named "Mutual Assured Destruction" (MAD, for short). Nuclear war was deemed "unthinkable."

Strategists on both sides now seem convinced that nuclear weapons differ from conventional arms mainly in degree. This is an intolerable notion. In the nuclear age, war cannot be considered, as it was in Clausewitz's classic formulation, "the continuation of politics by other means."

THE PACIFIST IMPULSES spreading through Western democracies have bred an understandable mistrust of technology which has turned the introduction of new weapon systems into ideological confrontations. Precautionary responses carry a high political price as the universal distaste for militarism grows. Dr. Lawrence

Martin, Vice-Chancellor of the University of Newcastle-upon-Tyne, in England, has described the diverging paths of technological advance and public opinion.

Not since the demise of "massive retaliation" has it been seriously argued that nuclear weapons alone can deliver security. Some of the most important theoretical and practical questions therefore concern the interface between the nuclear and the conventional. Here the trends are ambiguous. Technology, with increased accuracy making smaller nuclear yields more effective, yet with the same accuracy and novel designs also increasing the efficacy of conventional devices, is tending to blur the distinction between nuclear and conventional so far as purely military functions are concerned. The public and the politicians, however, alarmed to some extent by this very trend – making the world safe for nuclear war – increasingly demand a sharper division, as exemplified most recently by the call for a NATO policy of no first use. Few strategists – though quite a lot of taxpayers – deny the desirability of stronger NATO conventional forces, but as a panacea it is a rather tired prescription with a long history of not being filled.

THE PROSPECT OF A MASSIVE NUCLEAR EXCHANGE that would claim at least 300 million lives in its first half hour is beyond comprehension. As John Kenneth Galbraith has pointed out: "Not even the most passionate ideologue will be able to tell the ashes of Capitalism from those of Communism – for, among other reasons, he too will be dead."

The sheer madness of such a scenario – the nuclear rockets in their silos, the buttons ready to be pushed – makes it difficult to view either of the superpowers dispassionately.

Above and beyond the possibility of a nuclear war breaking out as a deliberate policy initiative by one of the superpowers, is the increasing probability of an accident. The recent film *War Games*, in which a schoolboy almost triggers a third world war by cracking air defence computer codes, is no Hollywood fantasy. It not only could happen, it *has* happened. A United Press International story out of Milwaukee, on August 12, reported that ten young-sters who had seen the film were being investigated by the FBI for using their home computers to gain access to a computer hooked up to the top-secret Los Alamos lab where scientists developed the nuclear and hydrogen bombs. At another, even more serious level, a Congressional Report of senators Barry Goldwater and Garry Hart to the Committee on Armed Services, tabled on October 9, 1980, described how a major alert had been set off at the North American Defence Command on November 26, 1979. The false alert, lasting six full minutes, was triggered when a technician mis-takenly mounted a training tape of a Soviet attack on an American military computer.

During a typical eighteen-month period, the NORAD system reported 151 false alarms, 4 of which (including the accidental tape insertion) were serious enough to place B-52 bomber crews and intercontinental ballistic missile units on an increased state of alert. In one incident, on October 5, 1960, NORAD's central defence room received a top priority warning from the Thule, Greenland, Ballistic Missile Early Warning Systems (BMEWS) station indica-ting that a missile attack had been launched against the United States. Roy Slemon, the Canadian air marshal in command, under-took verification, which after 15 to 20 minutes showed the warning to be false. The radar beams had echoed off the moon.

Twice during 1971 Submarine Emergency Communications Transmitter (SECT) buoys, accidentally released from US Polaris nuclear missile submarines, signalled that the submarines had been sunk by enemy action.

These mix-ups were cleared up – in time. But the world was at risk.

No information is available on such near-accidents in the USSR, but the Russians must have similar problems.

Quite apart from accidents, another seriously destabilizing fac-tor in today's world is the mental health of the soldiers charged with handling nuclear weapons on both sides. Once again, no exact data is available about the Soviets, but Professor Lloyd J. Dumas, a political economist at the University of Texas who has studied the issue, notes that "alcohol dependency in the Soviet military is certainly as high as the 18% some analysts estimate for the U.S. military and perhaps as high as 30% or more. Anecdotal reports persist of consumption by Soviet military personnel of eau de cologne, brake fluid, aircraft windshield de-icer and even of a process whereby shoe polish is spread on bread set in the sun and then the lower part of the bread, into which the alcohol is distilled, is consumed. There is little direct information available, but there is some. For example, a former Soviet army lieutenant stationed in the Ukraine in the mid-1970s reports: 'In our unit, 8 men once drank large quantities of the anti-freeze used in the truck engines. All of them were badly poisoned. One soldier died, two went blind, the rest were in a serious condition and had to be taken to hospital.'"

In the United States, the Pentagon operates a secret annual review called the "Personnel Reliability Program" to assess the mental and physical status of the hundred thousand troops who have daily access to nuclear weapons. In 1975, 5,128 personnel were removed from access to nuclear weapons for what was described as "significant physical, mental or character traits or aberrant behaviour, substantiated by competent medical authority. (Eight hundred and eighty-five were reassigned for evidence "of a contemptuous attitude toward the law"; 350 for court-martial or civil convictions; and 828 for "negligence" – a frightening word in this context.) One USAF doctor described the case of a psychotically depressed maintenence sergeant at a nuclear facility who had rigged a pistol to fire off a nuclear warhead as part of his personal suicide plan – though it wasn't clear whether the contraption would actually have worked. Three men working at the top-secret section in which American nuclear war plans are maintained were arrested for possession and sale of marijuana and LSD. One Army code specialist, Donald Meyer, admitted at the time that he used hashish two or three times every four hours daily for the more than two years he worked at a missile base in Germany. "Missile soldiers were sometimes high when they attached nuclear warheads to the missiles," went his 1974 story in the *Milwaukee Journal*, and "so were the soldiers who connected the two pieces up to make the missile operational."

According to Forest S. Tennant, who studied drug abuse in the American army while stationed in Germany, forty-six per cent of a sample of recruits reported using an illegal drug at least once, and sixteen per cent reported using such drugs more than three times a week. "Lysergic acid diethylamide (LSD) is abundantly available. Adverse psychiatric reactions to LSD have accounted for the majority of drug-related hospitalizations since 1968, although opiates currently cause the highest number of hospitalizations," he reported. LSD causes a characteristic psychosis for eight to ten hours. During this time an individual may suffer attacks of panic and paranoia. Addictive agents such as narcotics create the so-called purposive syndrome in which all behaviour becomes oriented towards seeking the addicting agent. An addicted soldier, and the system of weapons control, is vulnerable to subversion by anyone offering an opium dream to "treat" drug withdrawal.

Dr. Henry David Abraham, an American physician who has specialized in the field, diagnoses the problem.

Safeguards have been designed to thwart a deranged individual from launching missiles without authorization. For example, there is the concept of a "permissive action link," a control feature over nuclear launchers that prevents individuals from acting singly to launch a nuclear attack. An ICBM, for example, requires two keys that must be turned within a few seconds of each other, but which are spaced too far apart in the silo for a single person to turn them. While this system may well serve to reduce the chance of a single psychotic launching a missile, it does not prevent two psychotics from joining forces and acting on a shared delusion. This psychiatric syndrome, the *folie à deux*, comes about in a pair of individuals who share close daily contact with each other. One of them, clinically called the inductor, suffers from a delusional disorder into which the inductee is drawn. Such a delusion may often be of a paranoid nature. That more than one individual working in concert may discharge nuclear weapons is a point made by a former missileer, who stated that four members of a Minuteman squadron could without authorization begin World War III.

General George Blanchard, an American Senior Field Commander in Europe, once estimated that eight per cent of all GIs stationed on the continent are into hard drugs. One of the main problems seems to be sheer boredom. Ted Wye, a former air force deputy missile combat crew commander, reported on life in the hardened silos of the land-based missile force (in a supplement to *Air Force* magazine):

> There is no entertainment to pass the time and relieve the monotony. Except for an occasional alarm, a capsule tour consists of hours of quietude. . . .Under near-maddening conditions of isolation, boredom and frustration, missile crews develop a different perspective than superiors. . . .The idle time on a missile officer's hands must be similar to a prisoner's life in solitary confinement . . . only . . . there are two of you. A crew member tries not to think about his ultimate responsibility, which could lead to the killing of millions of people. . . . He is not supposed to have a conscience. . . . He learns to contrast his personal feelings and the role he is expected to play, unquestioningly and automatically. The hypocrisy of this game he's playing creates a feeling of disinvolvement. He tends to see his personal life and official life as totally separate; the launch officer becomes schizoid."

Nor is the nuclear military immune from the potentially devastating effects of stress and another kind of isolation at the top of the chain of command. According to Watergate reporters Bob Woodward and Carl Bernstein, in the final days of his presidency, Richard Nixon, Commander-in-Chief of the American Armed Forces, showed considerable signs of emotional instability and general loss of control, and was heard to mutter: "Why, I can go into my office and pick up the telephone, and in twenty-five minutes seventy million people will be dead."

THE NATURE OF THE VIETNAM WAR permanently tarnished the international idealism once claimed by the United States. The Soviet Union's status as a superpower is based mainly on the level of its defence spending which (in terms of the equivalent dollar expenditure) has been running forty per cent ahead of that of the United States. Since the thirteenth century, when Tartar hordes from Mongolia (Moslems by persuasion) invaded Russia in a bloodtide of exuberant carnage, war and its barbarous legacies have caused the Russians to regard most foreigners as people either to be feared or subjugated. Russian history is a chronology of horror, violence, and intrigue. Ivan the Terrible, a sixteenth-century czar who came by his nickname honestly, had seven wives – each of whom was poisoned by ambitious noblemen who didn't want him to have an heir. Memories of the Napoleonic Wars and Adolf Hitler's campaign (in which twenty-three million Russians were massacred) remain raw and vivid. In Moscow, newlyweds, fresh from their marriage ceremonies, feel compelled to place part of their wedding bouquets on the Tomb of an Unknown Soldier in the Alexandrovsky Gardens alongside the Kremlin wall. In Leningrad (which suffered the most grievous casualties), acres of hummocks in the Piskarevka Cemetery bulge with so many victims of Hitler's siege that each mass grave is marked simply by the year of death – 1941, 1942, 1943. One can still see old men in the street cafes moving salt shakers and cutlery as they refight the Great Patriotic War.

The 1917 Russian Revolution gave birth to a form of political mysticism that created the most powerful secular religion the world has ever known. It has its own bible (*Das Kapital*), saints (Marx, Engels, and Lenin), and apostles (the current Politburo).

It takes a hardened demon-hunter of Alexander Solzhenitsyn's stamp to extrapolate a doomsday scenario in which the Kremlin is seen as plotting the conquest of the planet. But it requires little more than a careful reading of the actual events since the Second World War to draw some less dramatic but only slightly less worrying conclusions. George F. Kennan, who has been studying and taking part in American-Soviet affairs for over half a century, has constantly urged Western governments to understand the traditionally threatened state of mind of the Russian people and their leaders. "As this leadership looks abroad, it sees more dangers than inviting opportunities. Its reactions and purposes are therefore much more defensive than aggressive. It has no desire for any major war, least of all for a nuclear one. It fears and respects American military power even as it tries to match it, and hopes to avoid a conflict with it."

To provide insulation from ideological currents contrary to

their own flowing outside their borders, the Communists have constantly sought to strengthen both the physical and spiritual dykes around Mother Russia. Unlike the Americans, who have influenced much of the world by the dynamism of their consumer-oriented economy – transplanting their values to the outer reaches of civilizations through the fiscal leverage of Wall Street and the marketing wizardry of Madison Avenue – the Soviets have a system and society neither envied nor emulated. There was a time, during the 1920s and 1930s, when appeals to the egalitarian impulses of subjugated and exploited work forces could work miracles – indeed 121 branches of the Communist party, mostly born in those decades, still exist. But as communism has progressively lost its power to compel belief, the Kremlin has resorted to its only other option: attempting to change the balance of world power through the force of arms. Armed proxy states such as East Germany, Cuba, and Vietnam have injected a strong Soviet presence into the Third World.

Few objective observers of the balance of terror that has come to constitute East-West relations share Ronald Reagan's obsession with a world-wide Communist conspiracy. But it's hard not to acknowledge the direct and indirect applications of Soviet power that have characterized the past two-and-a-half decades: Hungary (1956), Czechoslovakia (1968), Yemen (1967), Somalia (1970), Angola (1975), Ethiopia (1977), Afghanistan (1979), and Poland (1981).

ONE OF THE MOST PECULIAR probes by the USSR has been the continued appearance of their submarines in Swedish waters. According to the June 23, 1983, issue of the *Wall Street Journal*, "Swedish officials have concluded that the recent submarine incursions are part of a crash effort by the Soviet Union to update its battle plans for conventional war in Europe. The Swedes aren't pretending that war is imminent, but they do believe that the Soviets are testing Swedish defences in order to develop detailed war plans." American strategists have pointed out that despite Sweden's neutrality, in the event of another war, Soviet troops and planes from the Baltic coast and the Murmansk area would try to swarm across Sweden into neighbouring Norway, because Norway's western coastline makes that NATO nation the key to controlling the flow of Soviet submarines into the North Atlantic.

A Swedish royal commission recently reported that there have been more than forty submarine incursions into Swedish territorial waters during 1982 and the first six months of 1983, many of them near major cities, strategic inlets, and sensitive naval bases. These adventures have backfired on the Kremlin by dramatically altering Sweden's national will. The Swedish government plans to spend an extra $32 million for submarine defences over the next five years and will go ahead with a new jet aircraft, the Jas. Public opinion has become more defence-minded: in a recent poll, sixty per cent thought that Swedish defences would help keep the country out of war; in 1977, sixty-one per cent took the opposite view. In the new poll, forty-six per cent said the defence effort was not great enough, compared with twenty per cent in 1982.

THE MUTUAL SUSPICIONS of East and West inevitably translate themselves into generations of new weapons. Sir Arthur Conan Doyle, the creator of Sherlock Holmes, noted long ago that armies are always ready and eager to use each new piece of technology. He described how English longbows spelled the end of the heavily armoured cavalry of the Middle Ages, just as cannon presaged the end of the bow.

The most deeply disturbing new element of the East-West confrontation is that both sides have been hinting that nuclear war on a limited scale could not only be fought, but won. This ultimate fallacy is based, at least in part, on the continuing erosion of the West's strategic position. NATO is outmanned and outgunned by the Warsaw Pact countries in every category.

According to London's *Sunday Times*, the newest Soviet super-weapon is an armed helicopter called the Hind — a tank destroyer that can strike with devastating effect far behind front lines. It carries sixteen laser-guided anti-tank missiles which, like the French Exocet, automatically home in on their targets. The USSR is reported to be turning out these new units, invented a decade ago, at the astonishing rate of one per day. The West has nothing

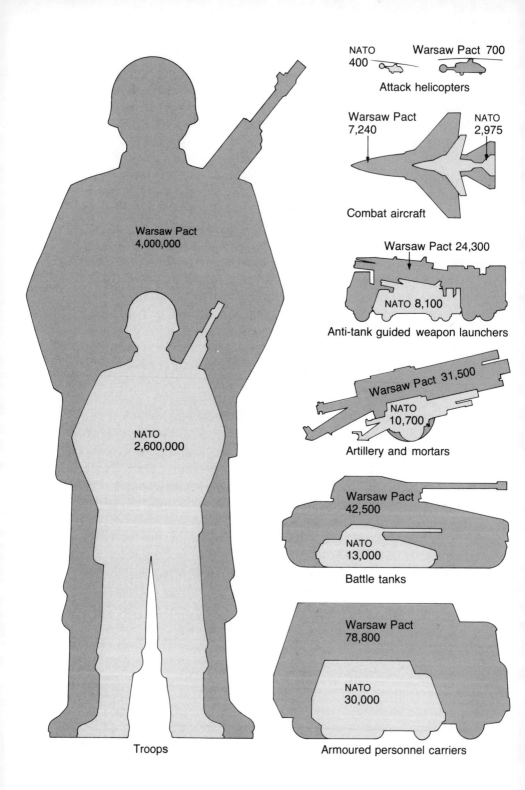

NATO 400

Warsaw Pact 700

Attack helicopters

Warsaw Pact 7,240

NATO 2,975

Combat aircraft

Warsaw Pact 24,300

NATO 8,100

Anti-tank guided weapon launchers

Warsaw Pact 31,500

NATO 10,700

Artillery and mortars

Warsaw Pact 42,500

NATO 13,000

Battle tanks

Warsaw Pact 78,800

NATO 30,000

Armoured personnel carriers

Warsaw Pact 4,000,000

NATO 2,600,000

Troops

to match the Hind. The roughly comparable but inferior American Apache helicopter is scheduled for delivery in 1989 but its dozen or so test models have not been particularly effective.

The key to NATO's hopes of countering any conventionally armed Soviet assault on Western Europe is the speed with which North American reinforcements could be brought across the Atlantic to provide the fire and manpower that might dictate a pause before forcing an escalation to nuclear weapons. NATO estimates indicate that 1.4 million men and 14 million tons of supplies would have to be moved across the ocean during the first ninety days of fighting, just to hold the line. This would require two thousand merchant ships – an average of three hundred and fifty cargo vessels at sea at any one time – in need of naval protection.

That is why Moscow has given such high priority to a massive maritime buildup. During the past two years the Soviets have launched forty major new surface vessels – plus a new nuclear-powered submarine every month, according to the authoritative *Jane's Fighting Ships*. Russian underwater strength is estimated at 377 first-line submarines, the largest of them being the 33,000-ton Typhoon-class, the length of two football fields. The size of a full-scale aircraft carrier, the Typhoon has a revolutionary double-skinned hull design which gives it the ability to fire its twenty SSN-X-20 missiles simultaneously, and immediately reload for another salvo. Each missile is armed with a dozen warheads that can be lobbed into North American targets over the North Pole.

The Soviets' titanium-hulled Alfa-class submarine has been tracked underwater at speeds up to forty-two knots. It can turn 180 degrees in ninety seconds and is capable of diving deeper than any other warship. A new, yet-to-be-designated Soviet submarine is reported to be capable of travelling at sixty-three knots on unconventional fuels, using the science known as "cryogenics." The Americans don't know how to make submarines go nearly that fast; some new Russian models can even outrun American torpedoes.

The most powerful element in the Soviet surface fleet is the Kirov-class nuclear-powered cruiser, which carries five attack helicopters and ninety-six missiles in rechargeable launchers, some with projectiles that travel at six times the speed of sound.

The American navy's modern underwater craft can't boast such sophistication, but they're deadly weapons just the same. Every one of the new $1.5 billion Trident II subs carries 224 nuclear warheads – each capable of frying a Russian city centre. Under Ronald Reagan's $1.8 trillion re-armament program, the American navy will have thirty Trident IIs in service by 1990.

"The Soviet Maritime threat," Admiral Sir Henry Leach, formerly Britain's First Sea Lord, has commented, "is formidable and continues inexorably to increase. The real cause of anxiety is in the relative rate of improvement in Soviet naval forces – it is more than double that of the West. This buildup goes way beyond any reasonable requirements for defence and can only be interpreted as being offensive. For reasons of geography, if the West were denied use of the sea-lanes, it would be a catastrophe; if the Soviets were to be similarly denied, it would merely be an inconvenience."

CHAPTER THIRTEEN

Killing Time in NATO

"Peaceful co-existence is designed to achieve global military supremacy in 1985, by which time the forces of world socialism will be in a position to dictate their will to the remnants of capitalist power in the West."

LEONID BREZHNEV

I N A NONDESCRIPT BUILDING on the outskirts of Brussels, hurriedly erected after Charles de Gaulle expelled NATO from France in 1966, generals and admirals in mufti meet with their diplomatic brothers-in-arms to plan what they describe to themselves as "the multilateral defence of our way of life."

They have been sitting out the twentieth century at NATO for thirty-four years now, these comfortable men with clipped moustaches and three-piece suits. Should a war come, they will be at the forefront of planning the West's strategy. Even though they hold the seasons in their hands the impression at NATO is that war and peace have been reduced to a set of gamesman's rules, like the code of an old and fashionable club.

Even if Western Europe's youths are in the streets marching against them, the men who run NATO have managed to hold the Alliance together for more than three harsh decades, granting the continent its longest period of peace this century. No multinational defensive alliance in history has lasted as long. Even the loose systems by which peace was maintained in the past – the Congress of Vienna, for example, or the Bismarck-Disraeli arrangements of the late nineteenth century – didn't prove nearly as durable. NATO's main purpose is to provide a collective defence arrangement by which aggression against the territory of any member state of the Alliance is regarded as an attack on all others. At the same time, NATO connotes a sense of a wider community, of shared interests, and political organization.

By the early 1980s, the Alliance was facing an unprecedented crisis in self-confidence. For the first time since it was forged at the end of the 1940s – at least partly the brainchild of Canada's Lester B. Pearson – NATO had decisively lost its military superiority to the Warsaw Pact countries.

Gone was any certainty among its dozen European members that either the conventional arms available or America's nuclear umbrella could vouchsafe the continent's security. The professional bravado of the generals, admirals, and ambassadors who run the Alliance's bureaucratic fortress in Belgium was being diluted by a *fin-de-siècle* fatalism, the distinct impression that they were caught in the tightening noose of circumstances beyond their control.

Despite its inferiority to that of the Soviets, the NATO arsenal of men and weapons remains impressive, with its standing armies, wings of tactical jets, and fleets of warships. "But in relative terms, the balance of conventional military power between NATO and the Waraw Pact is swinging in favour of the Soviets," insists Admiral Sir James Eberle, until recently one of the Alliance's three military chiefs and now in charge of the Royal Navy's Home Command. "If we allow this trend to continue, then we should recognize our military commanders will have less flexibility in executing conventional strategies and the nuclear threshold [that point at which NATO either has to go nuclear or surrender] will fall."

With some exceptions, NATO members have stuck to their pledges of raising their defence spending to three per cent of their gross national product. But the pace of Soviet rearmament has accelerated so remarkably in recent years that the Warsaw Pact countries' firepower now outnumbers NATO's by margins that would almost guarantee the West losing any armed confrontation. "Even with the assured 48 hours' warning time," says Nils Orvik, director of the Centre for International Relations at Queen's University in Kingston, Ontario, "NATO would lose. The mobilization of NATO reserves forces would most likely require too much time to become effective. In crude and harsh terms, the choice would then be either to accept conventional defeat or escalate to the nuclear level."

Sharing the Defence Burden - 1982

Total armed forces as per cent of work force

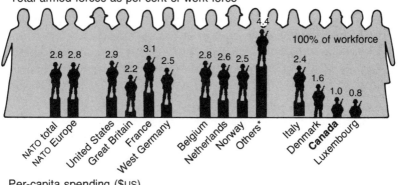

Per-capita spending ($US)

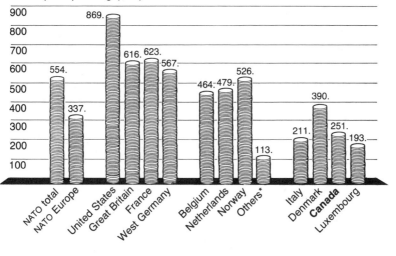

Defence as per cent of GNP

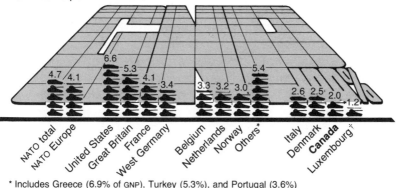

* Includes Greece (6.9% of GNP), Turkey (5.3%), and Portugal (3.6%)
† In 1983 Luxembourg's defence spending as a % of GNP moved ahead of Canada's.

133

This disparity between East and West on the NATO front, which guarantees escalation to a nuclear exchange, has been widening at an alarming rate. The Warsaw Pact, for example, has added 10,000 tanks to its forces opposite Western Europe, to reach a total of 42,500, while NATO tank levels have remained unchanged. The Soviets command 2,700 more jet fighters than the Alliance.

But the most dramatic decline in NATO's superiority has been at sea. In 1970, NATO had 38 attack and anti-submarine warfare carriers. By 1982, the number was down to 15. In 1970, the number of fleet escorts declared to NATO was 550. Now it is 335. A decade ago, NATO had 155 ocean-going conventional submarines. Now it has 57. Since 1970 the number of NATO maritime patrol aircraft has shrunk from 671 to 283. In 1970, the number of Soviet nuclear-powered submarines was twenty more than those of NATO. Today the lead has nearly doubled to thirty-eight. During the same interval, the Soviet fleet of conventionally powered submarines has grown to four times the number of NATO's. Since 1970 the number of Soviet maritime patrol aircraft has increased from 125 to 180. In 1970, the Warsaw Pact had 490 long-range aircraft capable of attacking NATO warships in the Norwegian Sea. They now have 620. In 1970, NATO nations had 560 mine-countermeasures vessels. This number has been reduced by more than forty per cent. In 1970, four major amphibious ships were available for the lift of NATO's amphibious force. Now there are none. In the same period, the Soviets have doubled their amphibious lift capability.

NATO's confidence is further eroded by the fact that after more than three decades of trying, the Alliance still has not accomplished any significant weapons standardization. That failure means that in any conflict NATO's national forces could not resupply one another. Thirty-one different anti-tank weapons are currently in use, for example, along with twenty-three varying tactical combat aircraft and forty-one types of naval guns. One expert estimates that NATO wastes at least $11 billion a year in equipment overlap alone.

NATO strategy was originally based on a "sword and shield" concept. Its armies were to have been built up to 90 divisions, a force powerful enough to hold back the first push by the 175 divisions the Soviets maintained west of the Ural Mountains. Behind this "shield" stood the "sword" of the United States Air Force Strategic Air Command – prepared, if necessary, to back up NATO troops with attacks on the enemy's homeland. But the 90 divisions never materialized. France withdrew all but two of her divisions to the Algerian war, then pulled out altogether from military participation in NATO. The West Germans delayed their contribution. The British left a relatively small garrison on the continent. It soon became obvious that the NATO "shield" was little more than a glorified border patrol able merely to signal news of any Soviet attack.

At the ministerial conference in 1954, NATO's generals were told to draw up an alternative strategy based on a leveling-off of defence expenditures by members of the Alliance and the adoption of tactical nuclear weapons. They produced a foot-thick secret document called MC-70 which recommended "graduating the West's deterrent." This meant NATO armies would create a secondary deterrent – strong enough to discourage the Soviets from attacking Europe with their overwhelming land forces, but not powerful enough, if such an attack came, to fry the world in a nuclear exchange. This plan was adopted in December 1957, though few non-military strategists had much faith in the distinction between tactical and strategic atomic weapons. The generals argued that tactical nuclear weapons were the only way of taking war back to the battlefield. What terrified opponents of the tactical warheads was that their adoption, for the first time in history, placed two nuclear armies face to face. "Commanders will always tend to use every weapon they possess rather than risk their troops being overrun," the British strategist B. H. Liddell Hart noted. Under this NATO strategy, no single individual would have to assume the awesome responsibility for making the decision that would set off the Third World War. Battles would grow out of border incidents, decisions would follow one another; at no specific point would the obstacle of human conscience intrude. NATO's decision-making is like a clock mechanism which governments wind and rewind with the support of lagging public opinion, but whose actual motion, like that of time, eludes intervention.

During the late 1960s, NATO developed yet another new strategy called "flexible response." Instead of trying to rely entirely on the threat of massive nuclear retaliation to deter all possible kinds of Soviet attack, NATO decided that it must be able "to respond flexibly." This did not require matching the Soviets weapon for weapon, but it did mean having a reasonably large and varied armoury, including smaller nuclear weapons that could be used against military targets on or behind the battlefield, known as "theatre nuclear weapons." The aim of all this was to convince the Russians that NATO would always have both the will and the ability to go on resisting any attack rather than accept defeat. These are concepts that lie behind the 1979 NATO decision to base American Pershing II ballistic missiles and ground-launched cruise missiles in Europe.

An approach benignly called "seamless deterrence" has become NATO's official doctrine. Stripped of its military jargon, this means that NATO's response to any Soviet aggression, conventional or not, would rapidly and *automatically* escalate into nuclear exchange.

Pushed by what former Minister of National Defence, Gilles Lamontagne, called "the astonishing and alarming growing power of the Soviet Union," NATO reluctantly accepted the dictum that it has to demonstrate its willingness to use nuclear weapons if there is to be any hope of preventing a Third World War. "We must," insisted NATO Secretary-General Joseph Luns, "keep Moscow in uncertainty about whether or not we will use these weapons. But the launching of nuclear missiles can never be completely automatic because both the USSR and America know that if they escalate, within eight minutes the other side will reply in kind – and that might be the end of their civilizations."

DESPITE SUCH DISCLAIMERS, Nino Pasti, an Italian senator and a former Deputy Supreme Commander for NATO nuclear affairs, has complained that "Europe is to be transformed into a 'nuclear Maginot Line' for the defence of the United States."

Any real threat of war would quickly reveal NATO's fatal flaw: all major policy decisions have to be unanimous, and every member has an equal vote. It takes a considerable leap of imagination to suppose that, for instance, a future Chancellor of West Germany would agree to launch the first nuclear weapon from his home ground against East Germany – knowing what the likely retaliation would be.

Any hope of halting a nuclear exchange at some level of sanity would depend on world leaders being able to keep in constant touch with one another so that at the very least a format for bargaining would continue to exist. This brings up the vision, from dozens of bad novels and worse films, of a hyperventilating president of the United States tersely whispering into a red hotline telephone to his opposite number in the Kremlin. The facts are slightly more prosaic and a lot more frightening. NATO's confidential records show that in 1964 a thief snipped out a six-metre section of the line near Helsinki; twelve months later a fire in a manhole at Rosedale, Maryland, cut the circuit again, as did a careless farmer ploughing his fields in northern Finland, and a Russian ship that ran aground on the east coast of Denmark. At one point, a Finnish postal workers' strike put civilization's "hotline" out of commission for several hours. The only alternative has been to hook it up through communications satellites, but they may be among the first victims of a nuclear exchange.

Paradoxically, the greatest long-term threat to NATO comes not from its enemies but from within. The tidy allegiances of the post-war world are beginning to disintegrate, leaving most Western European statesmen, in the late Aneurin Bevan's memorable phrase, "writhing on the twin hooks of conscience and expediency." Even if *The Economist*'s recent charge that "the Atlantic Alliance is in the early stages of what could be a terminal illness" is too harsh a judgement, the centrifugal forces tearing at NATO are growing stronger. No alliance can prosper when its members hold such radically differing views of the adversary it was originally established to fight.

The consequences of the widening gulf in the European and American perceptions of the Kremlin's intentions are easier to recognize than to explain. It is less a difference of knowledge than of intuition, more the legacy of experience than any deep philosophical rift.

For most Europeans, history isn't something invented at White House press conferences or State Department "deep-backgrounders." Europe breathes its history; cities and streets are haunted by ghosts of vanished realms. A wall at Hougoumont, near Waterloo, still bears the pockmarks of the cannon balls that marked the end of Napoleon's dreams of empire in the bloody summer of 1815. Placed inconspicuously among the scars is a modest plaque to the British Coldstream Guard Regiment that helped liberate the area, two wars later, in 1944.

Nothing in Europe is really new. In 1982 a University of London professor published a book titled *Reform and Insurrection in Poland.* It deals with the troubles of 1856. More than a century ago, the Ruhr steelmasters were supplying Russia when Germany was still part of Bismarck's proud empire and the czars were safely ensconced in St. Peterburg's Winter Palace. Almost everything on the continent is based on habit and strict observance of precedence so that, for example, the mourning pennant flown by bereaved Belgian barge captains who are Catholics is a recognized flag quite different from that of bereaved Belgian barge captains who happen to be protestants.

The same intense delicacy of grief and remembrance that keeps Buchenwald and Dachau from European lips will not permit the notion of a nuclear war to be dignified with serious discourse. The grand notion represented by such devalued words as "peace" and "free enterprise" may still be able to rouse Americans to arms, but Europeans know that a Third World War will find them in the frontline trenches yet again, their cities razed to moonscapes.

Felipe Gonzalez, the leader of Spain's Socialist Party, has summed up the feelings of most young Europeans. "They believe all superpowers are alike. They didn't live through the experience of having the U.S. as a liberator. They are in a debate that began with the Vietnam War. I think that the U.S. is not sensitive to this change of opinion, one which forgets the role of liberator."

What few American diplomats appreciate is the continent's startling new demography. Fully half of contemporary Europe's citizens were born after the end of the Korean War, the last conflict in which the United States could claim moral superiority. The generation of leaders now moving into power in most of Europe has no memory of the Americans as sponsors of the Marshall Plan or as Cold War heroes. Their attitude toward the Americans was spawned by television coverage of wisecracking GIs shooting peasants in black pyjamas in the rice paddies of Vietnam. Apart from their revulsion, they ask themselves why North Vietnam was never conquered; why Fidel Castro continues to thumb his nose at the White House; why the Americans were so helpless in the face of Iran's revolutionaries; why Washington supports a repressive junta in El Salvador; why NATO did nothing when Hungary was invaded in 1956, Czechoslovakia in 1968, or when Poland was humiliated in 1981.

These are uncomfortable issues, not really resolved by Washington-inspired tallies of the Communists' overt conquests and their dismal record on human rights. The most thoughtful condemnation of communism's effects comes from the musings of French philosopher Raymond Aron, who questions the original Marxist vision by noting the existence of gulags. Writes Aron: "If the virtues of an economic regime are measured by its capability to answer the wishes of the population, organize the rational allocation of resources and efficiently produce the goods necessary to the physical and moral well-being of individual people, the Soviet experience remains the most spectacular failure in history."

That may be true. But it gives cold comfort to those Europeans convinced that American defence strategy remains predicated on the Clausewitzian doctrine of trading space for time, designed to protect their home territory by confining future hostilities to the battlegrounds of Europe – as was the case in two previous world wars. Even though this does not in fact reflect the military planning of either the Pentagon or NATO, most Europeans go to extraordinary lengths to provide rationales for Soviet transgressions, including the Kremlin's invasion of Afghanistan and the suppression of Poland's bid for liberalization.

Determined to establish their own, rather than imported values, many Western Europeans no longer feel they have to choose between being beholden to either of the superpowers – and would dearly love to reject the influence of both.

Faced by what they regard as an obdurate abdication of responsibility by formerly dependable partners, the Americans accuse European politicians of "pre-emptive surrender" – a phrase intended to conjure up Neville Chamberlain and his umbrella. Secretary of Defence Caspar Weinberger has pointedly reminded

Western Europeans about the false prophets of the 1930s, who "dismissed as alarmist and warmongering the warnings of men like Winston Churchill, who saw the threat for the terrible danger it posed." NATO's main dilemma used to be the question of American credibility in European eyes; now the equation has been reversed. Europeans counter accusations that they have a "Munich mentality" with their "1914 analogy," which implies that war will come not through attempting to reach an accommodation with the Soviets, but as the result of mutual miscalculation and misunderstanding.

THIS DEBATE HAS CENTRED on the cruise and Pershing missiles due to be installed on NATO territory in late 1983. By Washington's count, the USSR already has in place 340 medium-range SS-20s, of which more than 250 are targeted on Western Europe. Each has the necessary range to reach any of Western Europe's capitals with three 150-kiloton, separately targeted warheads containing killing power thirty times that of the primitive atomic device that flattened Hiroshima. While the Soviets continue deploying two more of these missiles a month, the proposed NATO buildup of 572 Pershing II and cruise missiles would still leave NATO in an inferior position. By then, the USSR will have 750 or so SS-20s in place.

Although the Geneva disarmament talks aimed at dismantling this bristle of existing Russian missiles and preventing American retaliatory weapons from being installed are grinding on, no European is holding his or her breath. Negotiations on reduction of conventional forces between NATO and the Warsaw Pact are well into their ninth year, with no discernible progress. Georges Marchais, Secretary-General of the French Communist Party, probably summed up the chances for agreement most aptly when he dismissed the whole notion of detente as "the right of the imperialists to be beaten without a shot being fired."

The real nightmare of thoughtful NATO leaders is the prospect of what they refer to as the "self-Finlandization" of Western Europe. This pejorative label encapsulates Finland's dilemma. That country shares a 1,260-km border with the Soviet Union and has been vanquished by the Russians in 104 wars. Although Finland remains a vigorous democracy, its foreign policies are vetted by

Moscow. If carried to its logical conclusion, the Finlandization of the continent would mean that the local Soviet ambassador would become the most powerful presence in every Western European capital.

In military terms, the most Finlandized partner in NATO is Denmark, where Mogens Glistrup of the Progress Party, which holds the parliamentary balance of power, has advocated that the country's defence department be replaced by a telephone recording machine, with messages on it in Russian and English, repeating, "We surrender." (Even so, Denmark spends nearly twice as much for defence, on a per capita basis, as does Canada.)

It would make little sense for Soviet policy, no matter how ultimately triumphant, to inherit a Europe devastated by war. How much better (goes this reasoning) to neutralize the continent, turning Western Europe into a docile, industrially productive and supportive buffer zone, leaving Fortress America (and its last outpost, Canada) isolated and vulnerable. At a secret 1973 Warsaw Pact enclave in Prague, the late Leonid Brezhnev boasted that "peaceful coexistence is designed to achieve global military supremacy in 1985, by which time the forces of world socialism will be in a position to dictate their will to the remnants of capitalist power in the West." Certainly, such Finlandizing attempts to split the Old World from the New appear to be at the core of the Kremlin's current operational code.

If the Alliance is to regain its credibility as a deterrent, it must drastically increase its conventional military capabilities. As the Atlantic Institute of Canada recently pointed out:

If NATO is strong enough to hold Soviet-bloc forces for an extended period by conventional means, there will be time to test Soviet resolve, time to ascertain Soviet objectives and, most importantly, time for Alliance leaders to take the enormously difficult decision about whether to launch nuclear weapons at the enemy. Thus, the greater lead time will increase the credibility of the Alliance's nuclear deterrent so that the Soviet Union will be less likely to mount an attack in the first place. A stronger conventional capability should significantly reduce dissension among Alliance governments and the fears and doubts of Europeans regarding nuclear weapons. NATO would be much less likely to resort to the first use of nuclear weapons in the face of a Soviet conventional attack. Europeans would no longer confront the unnerving prospect of an almost immediate escalation to nuclear war. The dividing line between non-nuclear and nuclear weapons would be much clearer. Governments of the Alliance would be able to take defence policy decisions in a calmer, more rational atmosphere.

General Bernard Rogers, the Alliance's military commander, backed this doctrine at a press conference held in Brussels on September 28, 1982. He admitted that Western Europe could be defended without using nuclear weapons, providing NATO members agreed to quite modest improvements in the conventional forces available.

Implicit in this new approach was an informal offer: if nuclear disarmers would back him in asking for more and better conventional forces, Rogers could offer them the prospect of a higher nuclear threshold – as near to a non-first-use policy as NATO could get without actually saying so. "The anti-nuclear groups want the same thing as I do," he said.

He put the plan's cost at an extra one per cent on Alliance defence budgets, on average, for the rest of the 1980s. This is in addition to the three per cent growth (after allowing for inflation) which is already the nominal goal for all members, even if it's not being achieved by NATO partners now.

The key to Rogers' non-nuclear strategy is a combination of the latest reconnaissance technology – including the new TR1 aircraft, radar-equipped helicopters, AWACS, and satellites – with a range of highly accurate conventional missiles and guided weapons, including Pershing rockets and cruise missiles fitted with specialized non-nuclear warheads.

The fact that the man who is the supreme military commander of NATO has put forward a viable non-nuclear strategy for the Alliance demands immediate policy follow-up. Canada should be pushing hard to expand NATO's conventional military capabilities, so that the Alliance's dependence on nuclear weapons becomes a last – instead of a first – resort.

142

CHAPTER FOURTEEN

NATO's Lost Lamb

In terms of our proportionate NATO expenditures, we now rank at the bottom – except for Iceland, which has no armed forces at all.

ALONE AMONG NATO'S PARTNERS, Canada's membership in the Alliance serves a valuable symbolic function: it indicates a commitment to the defence of Western Europe by the only NATO member neither protecting its own soil nor involved in the superpower sweepstakes. Louis St. Laurent, who was prime minister when Canada helped establish NATO in the late 1940s, once patiently explained that our membership was comparable to an insurance premium: we paid our dues and in return were granted national protection. For twenty years, Canada was an important military presence in NATO, fielding a full brigade group that was acknowledged to be the best among such formations within the Alliance; our twelve squadrons of fighters were a significant part of Europe's air defence, and our fifty-two-ship navy included an aircraft carrier and destroyers with boilers that worked.

Then, in the 1960s, the wind-down began; by 1968 half our army brigade group and air squadron strength was cut. The naval element began its march to obsolescence.

The proportion of our gross national product spent on defence, ranked us, until recently, just ahead of Luxembourg, a tiny enclave with a population less than that of Winnipeg. No longer. The toy monarchy's 1983 defence budget ($42 million) is a larger percentage of their GNP than ours. In terms of our proportionate NATO expenditures, we now rank at the bottom – except for Iceland, which has no armed forces at all. Every NATO commander since Ike Eisenhower has praised the quality of Canadian troops, but the size of our commitment has become an embarrassment.

Canada's deliberate downplaying of its commitments is viewed by our NATO partners, many of whom themselves are not carrying a full load, as a retreat into isolationism. To Europeans concerned with defence of their continent, we have become a puzzle – careless free riders on their own and the American's military machine, yet self-righteous spouters trying to maintain our vaunted international piety intact.

Canada's schizophrenic policy (NATO if necessary but not necessarily NATO) is a betrayal of the very principal of mutual defence that prompted us to advocate the Alliance's formation in the first place. Other members of the Alliance, which has been the central vehicle for the conduct of Canadian foreign policy for more than two decades, now look upon our contribution as a symptom of how far our military prestige abroad has dropped. On January 10, 1946, General Eisenhower told the Canadian Club in Ottawa: "It is beyond the power of any man to add to the lustre of the military reputation established by the brave men and women of Canada who served with me in Europe." Lord Montgomery invariably referred to the Canadian army as "that splendid body of men." And Lieutenant-General Guy G. Simonds, a former Chief of the Canadian General Staff, summed up our achievements when he wrote, "The performance of Canadian fighting forces in two world wars contributed more to the development and international recognition of Canadian nationhood than any other single factor."

From 1951 to 1969, our Army brigade group was stationed near Soest, in northwest Germany, in what NATO planners called "a hinge position on the northern-central front of the main invasion route." Our air division in the Zweibrücken area, 163 miles south of Soest near the French border, had an attack function against Warsaw Pact targets. Now, our troops have been withdrawn to Lahr and Baden, to act as what's described as "primary reserve for counter attack and counter penetration." Whatever that means. Our air contingent has been reduced by half and the planes, CF-104s, have become not only dated but unsuitable to their new tactical support mission.

When Canada's phased reduction of its NATO contingent first became government policy in the spring of 1969, the issue was considered so controversial that instead of being announced at a formal meeting of NATO's Defense Planning Committee, Leo Cadieux, then Minister of National Defence, flew to Brussels – to break the news to a group of NATO ambassadors at a private reception in the apartment of Ross Campbell, Canada's chief delegate to NATO. One of the European delegates burst into tears; another protested our "unilateral breach of the principle of mutual security"; a third murmured darkly that Canada was a defector. "I have never been at a more emotional scene in all my life," Campbell later recalled.

Cadieux admitted his own personal disappointment in the policy, comparing it to a man who's been married for twenty years and asks for a divorce: "He goes to a lawyer and is told that he can't get a divorce simply on the basis of being fed up with his wife, so he stays with her in a divorce in spirit. But it just isn't the same: something's gone out of the relationship."

Pierre Trudeau's decision to emasculate the NATO commitment meant that we would stay in the Alliance, but our troops would be cut from ten thousand to five thousand (the original cut was to thirty-five hundred) and our six CF-104 squadrons would become three.

At the moment, Canada's NATO contribution consists of the Fourth Canadian Mechanized Brigade Group (really a mini-brigade) and the First Canadian Air Group, both stationed on the so-called Central Front. The former is based at Lahr, with one infantry battalion at Baden. Its peacetime strength is approximately thirty-four hundred. In theory at least, during a period of tension it could be augmented to about fifty-five hundred by having designated regular force personnel from Canada flown in to man equipment already in place.

Along NATO's northern flank, Canada's commitment includes a battalion group and a couple of squadrons of CF-5s. The land force has two deployment options: northern Norway, in the area of Troms, or the Baltic approaches, on the main Danish island of Zeeland. Plans call for this deployment to be carried out primarily by Canadian military airlift – with the heavy equipment required to sustain the force beyond a thirty-day period following by sea. (The 1st Battalion, Royal Canadian Regiment, in London,

Ontario, augmented by a battery of the 2nd Regiment, Royal Canadian Horse Artillery, in Petawawa, Ontario, are currently assigned to this task, as is 433 Squadron, based in Bagotville, Quebec.)

The most publicized – and least attainable – of Canada's NATO assignments is the Canadian Air-Sea Transportable Brigade Group (CAST). Since April 1977, the CAST Brigade Group has been allocated to northern Norway, its primary mission being to reinforce local Norwegian forces deployed to defend an attack through the Finnish wedge.

IN THE CURIOUS CALCULUS military strategists use to formulate their ideas, one of the few notions which finds universal acceptance is that while neither side in any East-West conflict could decisively "win" a European war by holding NATO's northern flank, either side would certainly "lose" by not maintaining control over the Greenland-Iceland-United Kingdom Gap.

The key nation in the defence of this essential stretch of geography is Norway. With Sweden and Finland bound to their own versions of neutrality, only Norwegian forces, or forces operating from its territory, could be used to bottle up Soviet fleets passing through the "choke points" they need to traverse before gaining unimpeded access to the North Atlantic.

An array of moored, underwater sonar detectors in the Bear Island Gap presently allows the Norwegians to monitor movement of Soviet submarines in the Barents Sea. Data from this network (collected near Tromso in northern Norway) as well as land-based radar, trace the activity of the Soviet Northern Fleet's air arm. Electronic intelligence-gathering facilities near the Soviet border listen in on the communications of the local naval headquarters. These intelligence assets provide NATO with substantial early warning signals.

Norway is a Western democracy pledged to the NATO concept of multi-lateral defence. Despite the strategic value of its real estate, Norway cannot expect to repulse attacks or defend itself exclusively with its own forces. The credibility of NATO's pledge to defend Norwegian territory in the event of East-West conflict depends on other members of the Alliance being willing to contribute troops.

Because Murmansk is the Soviet Union's only ice-free port to which access cannot easily be blocked, the Soviets have established in the area just across the Norwegian border the world's largest naval concentration – the Northern Fleet contains nearly two-thirds of the Soviet Union's retaliatory submarine-launched nuclear strike force, as well as major surface units. In the event of war, Norway would be vital for NATO conventional operations. Conversely, Soviet operations from Norwegian harbours and airfields could cut NATO's vital sea lanes between Europe and North America.

Norway has been a NATO partner since the Alliance's early days, but it has staunchly resisted accepting nuclear weapons or foreign bases on its soil in peacetime. As the only country in Western Europe that has a common frontier with the Soviet Union, Norway has a special problem. The Soviets might – understandably – react to the installation of missiles in Norway in the same way President Kennedy reacted to the placement of missiles in Cuba.

Norway's defence policy has until recently been based on a resolution passed by its Parliament on February 1, 1949: "The Norwegian government will not be party to any agreement with other states involving obligations on the part of Norway to make available to the armed forces of foreign powers bases on Norwegian territory, as long as Norway is not attacked or subject to the threat of attack."

The Soviets have exerted pressure on all Scandinavian countries, but on Norway in particular. The integration of Soviet and Finnish railway lines and the construction in Finland of highways pointing in the direction of Norway strongly suggest that, in the event of hostilities, the Soviets would strike fast to seize Norwegian ports and airfields, just as Hitler did in 1940.

As the result of these and other pressures, Norway has been trying to adjust its defences to changed conditions: it has agreed to accept limited stockpiles of arms and equipment for the NATO soldiers who would be used as reinforcements in the event of a Soviet attack, including most of the materiel for a battalion of Canadians.

Without a Canadian military presence, NATO assistance to Norway would be far less effective. The early arrival of a Canadian force would present the USSR with the prospect of an immediate escalation they might not otherwise have to contemplate.

But the deterrent value of the Canadian contribution would be due not to its size or military effectiveness, but to its instant availability *before* the actual outbreak of hostilities and its sustainable presence once it is in place. As presently set up, any potential Canadian reinforcements to Norway could not hope to meet either of these objectives. No one has actually said it in public, but the only way to get forty-five hundred of our boys in green across the Atlantic to Norway in time would be to load them aboard commandeered Air Canada jets. Their equipment, of course, would have to follow by sea. Canada's forces now have only twenty-seven slow-moving Hercules and five Boeing 707s for long-range transport, the latter capable of carrying a company of 210 men plus minimum supplies. Only the C-5 Galaxy transport is large enough to airlift the brigade's fighting hardware and only the USAF has C-5 Galaxies. Transport ships loaded with our troops' equipment could not make it through a screen of Soviet submarines.

As worthy as this Canadian contribution to the NATO deterrent may appear, neither our troops nor their equipment could safely cross the ocean in time to prevent any invasion of Norway.

The temptation to maintain this Norwegian NATO commitment is compelling. The defence of Norway is a cause Canadians could believe in. The problem is that we could not, even under the best circumstances, get our troops across the Atlantic in less than thirty days – by which time their presence would not deter anything.

Unlike the British, we have no deep-sea fleet to commandeer to transport our troops should we find ourselves in an equivalent to the Falklands emergency. There is a vague plan that calls for a wild dash across the Atlantic by Norwegian merchant ships or Danish ferries to pick our boys up, but nobody takes it seriously.

The CAST commitment, as desirable and attractive as it may be, should be phased out. As the Canadian Institute of Strategic Studies noted in its 1983 report:

The retention of this commitment is questionable on a number of grounds. Firstly, it means that other more important commitments such as Canada's maritime responsibilities are less likely to be adequately met. Secondly, even with increased manpower, the viability of the CAST commitment is questionable unless modern equipment for the brigade is pre-positioned in Norway and the necessary air- and sealift capability, now lacking, is provided. To fill these requirements would be extremely expensive. Thirdly, it is highly unlikely that in a time of high international tension a Canadian prime minister and cabinet would decide that the CAST group should be moved to Norway because of the escalatory impact such a movement might have. To attempt to deploy the CAST group after an outbreak of hostilities on the northern flank does not appear feasible. Finally, if there is an outbreak of hostilities in Europe, reinforcements for the brigade group in central Europe will be required if the conflict remains at the conventional level. On military grounds, it is not in Canada's interest to have two separate land commitments to the alliance in quite different geographical areas of the NATO region.

The other NATO land commitment is in Germany. It's a good question whether we are in a much better position to fulfill that Central Front pledge any better than the Norwegian one. As Rear-Admiral G. L. Edwards, when he was Director-General of Military Planning and Operations, Department of National Defence, pointed out: "Successful implementation of a conventional defence depends on the assured seaborne delivery of reinforcement and supply for both the military and civilian sectors. Indeed, NATO would have serious difficulty in holding Warsaw Pact aggression in Europe by conventional means unless the necessary men and supplies could cross the Atlantic from North America during the early stages of any crisis. The only way of transporting the majority of this quantity is by sea; aircraft can carry some of the tonnage, but over ninety per cent must go by ship."

That's why the state of Canada's navy becomes so significant. "Most of Canada's warships, their weapons and sensor systems," Edwards admitted, "were designed when the main target was the slow, conventional, snorkeling U-boat and when there was a negligible air and surface threat in the Atlantic. These old ships are only marginally effective against the fast, deep, missile-armed nuclear submarines. They also have a very limited defence against modern air, surface, or sub-surface launched missiles."

In other words, even if we did *try* to meet our existing NATO commitments, we could not do so.

CHAPTER FIFTEEN

True North: Not Strong and Free

Given any form of incursion by foreign troops into the Canadian Arctic – providing we ever found out about it – we could do nothing except send a Mountie out in a Skidoo to give out parking tickets.

THE ELUSIVE NATURE OF THE SEARCH for a Canadian identity has benefitted from having at least one peg on which its many would-be definers could safely agree: we are a northern people – our history has been the unique adventure of attempting to subjugate the sub-arctic furies of an untamed land. "Because of this origin in the northern frontier," wrote the historian W. L. Morton, "Canadian life to this day is marked by a northern quality. The line which marks the frontier from the farmstead, the wilderness from the baseland, the hinterland from the metropolis, runs through every Canadian psyche."

Given such inspiring genesis, the impartial outsider might suppose that some urgency would be allocated to the defence of our North, that we would care about what happens there and be concerned with maintaining sovereignty. Instead, Canada's North is the Earth's least effectively defended frontier. Given any form of incursion by foreign troops into the Canadian Arctic – providing we ever found out about it – we could do nothing except send a Mountie out in a Skidoo to give out parking tickets.

In the short term, the likelihood of an actual enemy invasion of our arctic territories may seem remote, but if we are to be persuasive even at a diplomatic level about our rights over our now greatly enlarged areas of claimed territory, we must be perceived by our neighbours, both friendly and unfriendly, to be establishing and claiming sovereignty. This apparent contradiction – that we should "defend" our North, even though no one is likely to attack it – is explained by John Gellner in his contribution to *The Arctic in Question.*

> If any proof were needed that the primary mission of the armed forces of a sovereign state is to support national policies and to assist in the achievement of national objectives – and that readiness to fight in a war is only a subsidiary function . . . it is provided by Canada's military engagement north of 60. Virtually no "defence" task in the literal sense of the word is involved. What is involved, is . . . the assertion of Canadian sovereignty over an area of land and sea of some one-and-a-half million square miles where the normal manifestations of national dominion are not, and cannot be, always present.

At the moment only 471 regular-force troops are stationed in our North – a territory of 8.7 million square kilometres – the largest military region in the world. Apart from the loosely organized straggle of reserve "Rangers" armed with hunting rifles, no one stands on guard for our North.

Precisely 1.6 times per month, an Armed Forces Aurora from either Comox or Greenwood lumbers across Canada's untended attic, but the effectiveness of such occasional surveillance can only be described as laughable. One example: back in 1943, a Nazi submarine crew slipped ashore on the northern coast of Labrador to erect a weather station. It went undetected until 1981, and was discovered then only because a curious German veteran had written the defence department in Ottawa to ask whatever happened to their installation. That such a substantial incursion could remain undetected for thirty-eight years in the treeless tundra is mute testimony to our neglect of the world's largest unguarded region.

Similarly, in August 1975, a Polish vessel found its way into the Northwest Passage. Its skipper sent a landing party ashore near Resolute to announce the expedition's presence. Despite an exhaustive three-day search, Canadian air patrols never did succeed in spotting them. On the other hand, in 1976, when a giant floe occupied by Russian scientists was discovered in Canadian waters, Defence Minister Barney Danson asserted Canadian sovereignty with the unique gesture of dropping a Christmas cake to the intruders.

Canada's Northern Regional Headquarters in Yellowknife has a total complement of seventy-five men who work out of a temporary building and have at their command an air fleet that consists in its obsolete entirety of two 1970-vintage propellor-driven Twin Otters. National Defence has built eight gravel-surfaced airfields — at Cape Dorset, Eskimo Point, Pangnirtung, Whale Cove, Pond Inlet, Frobisher, Spence Bay, and Alert. The sole significant military installation is at Alert but, because of its location, it can only be reached by Canadian aircraft if they stop to refuel at the American base in Thule, Greenland.

The only effective para-military presence in the Canadian North is the network of twenty-one outposts of the Distant Early Warning Line, built in 1955 by the United States. The Pinetree Line, which runs further south, from Holberg on Vancouver Island to Goose Bay in Labrador, has outlived its effectiveness. For one thing, some of its radar sets and computers are so antiquated that they still run off old-fashioned vacuum tubes — and the only suppliers which still manufacture replacements are two small factories located inside the Soviet Bloc.

Naval surveillance of the region does not exist. Admiral Dan Mainguy took the *Protector*, an unarmed supply ship, as far north as Lancaster Sound a few years ago, and naval vessels do occasionally venture into Hudson Bay, in summer, when there is barely an ice cube floating in the water. Canada's fledgling Coast Guard does, of course, have icebreakers, but they are mostly kept busy in the St. Lawrence. At the moment, the eastern entrance to the Northwest Passage is controlled by a system known as "Nordreg." What this consists of is the vague request that foreign vessels venturing through the Passage announce their intentions and report their locations by radio. Soviet and American nuclear submarines roam our North at will. The only Canadian fleet whose sailors know the Arctic belong to the oil companies exploring the Beaufort. Dr. Donald Shurman, head of the Department of History at the Royal Military College in Kingston, recently pointed out that "when we are at the stage in Canada where one or two oil companies have more knowledge about the nature of Canada's North and the ability to move around in it than the members of our Armed Forces, I think it is a serious situation."

In fact, the defence department obtains its most valuable data on what's going on in our Arctic from the Petroleum Institute in Houston, Texas, where the multi-nationals exploring the North store most of their facts.

There was a time when the Royal Canadian Navy had a proud ship, the six-thousand-ton HMCS *Labrador,* specifically designated for Northern patrols. Commissioned at Sorel in 1954, under the command of Captain O. C. S. Robertson, she headed North through Lancaster Sound to Resolute. Her official mission completed, the *Labrador*'s skipper decided to cable Ottawa on a Friday, just after Defence Headquarters had closed for the night, with the simple message: "Primary role completed. Returning to Halifax via Esquimalt." That was how Canada's first naval vessel transitted the Northwest Passage. Barely three years later, her new skipper, Captain T. H. Pullen, received a message from Ottawa announcing transfer of the *Labrador* out of the navy's service to the Department of Transport. She was never replaced and the navy now has zero ice-breaking capacity. "In my view," Pullen testified to a Parliamentary Committee in 1982, "the Department of National Defence is almost totally unaware of our maritime concerns in the Arctic. I said it before, and I will say it again, that the eyes of naval officers seem to be fixed permanently and firmly in an Easterly direction."

Canada's coat of arms proudly proclaims the motto: *A Mari usque ad Mare.* But in fact we face three, not two, oceans – and it is beneath the frigid waters off our north coast that half of Canada's potential oil and gas reserves are located. Most Canadians, if they think about it at all, believe that the waters within the Northern Archipelago are internal, and therefore belong to us.

The government has taken three major steps in the past decade which purport to establish our claims over arctic territories. These are: the *Arctic Waters Pollution Prevention Act* of 1972 which applies to all the waters of the arctic archipelago and extends a hundred miles seaward. It also applies to the continental shelf in the Arctic and to offshore drilling for oil and gas; the extension of

154

our territorial sea from three to twelve miles. This makes the North-West Passage a territorial, rather than an international, waterway; the declaration of the Exclusive Economic Zone which extends Canada's claim two hundred nautical miles seaward, and includes the right to manage resources, maritime pollution control, and marine scientific research. The fact is that none of these three claims are acknowledged by the USA, let alone by our northern neighbour, the USSR.

Dr. Harriet Critchley, program director of Northern Political Studies at the University of Calgary, has pointed out:

> We regard the Northwest Passage as a legal strait because at the two entrances, we have had strips of territorial sea since 1972, when we expanded our territorial sea [from 3] to 12 miles. That, according to international law, makes this a legal strait where we have the right to suspend innocent passage. The United States holds the position that the Northwest Passage is an *international* strait and that no coastal state has the right to suspend innocent passage in an international strait. Canada maintains that the Northwest Passage does not meet the definition of an international strait because the 18 or so transits of the Northwest Passage have all been experimental in nature and have not been used for regular commercial navigation. Therefore, we say the Northwest Passage does not meet, in a number of ways, the definition of an international strait. I believe the United States is continuing to hold its view because it is concerned that, if it grants the Canadian argument on the Northwest Passage, this might set a precedent for coastal-state rights over international waters, such as the Strait of Malacca, which are of considerable importance.

Dr. Critchley maintains that the enforcement of Canadian jurisdiction, hazy and disputed as it is, must fall upon the Canadian Armed Forces.

> While it can be argued either way as to our current capability to adequately detect such activities in the high Arctic and to enforce Canadian jurisdiction by such things as sovereignty flights and limited land capability, it is quite clear to me that we do not

have, nor do we appear to be planning to acquire, the capability that would be required within two decades. Part of that capability will have to include naval surface vessels that can sail into ice-infested waters but not necessarily ice-covered waters. Otherwise, what we are presenting to the world is a maritime nation which cannot operate its navy in a major portion of its coastal and ocean areas. This situation can be rather dangerous. We Canadians have a particular fondness for and mythological view of the Arctic. Others, when they look at our capability and see the low priority associated with Arctic matters and Arctic policy, can be forgiven if they doubt that we have this care about our own Arctic. When others take certain actions based on Canada's lack of capability and interest, we are unpleasantly surprised. I can give you one example of that: the reaction in this country to the voyages of the *Manhattan*. Our lack of capability and apparent lack of interest lead other states, be they friends or potential enemies, to underestimate or completely misread the potential Canadian reaction to any incidents or crises that will accompany increased maritime activity in Canada's high Arctic.

SOVEREIGNTY IS NOT the only thing we must be in a position to defend in our arctic territories. There is also oil. Even if the already geologically-mapped resources are considered, the North contains the world's largest pool of untapped energy wealth.

Looking at the world scene, one certain prediction can be made: another Middle East war will break out. When this occurs, the oil resources in our North will become much more valuable.

George Ignatieff, the distinguished Canadian diplomat who has represented Canada at many of the major international conferences, has analyzed the changing factors that are making the strategic value of the arctic regions increasingly important. In addition to the oil, he notes the build up of the Soviet navy in this northern area, and the technological developments that have altered defence thinking: "When NORAD was founded, the principal concern was the threat of Soviet long-range bombers using air routes across the Arctic to attack targets in the continental United

States. Now the development of mobile land-based nuclear-carrying missiles and submarine-launched missiles with intercontinental range, together with air-launched missiles from aircraft with refuelling capacities, all point to the fact that the High Arctic should increasingly be the focus of NATO and NORAD concern."

The notion of establishing an Arctic Command to defend the northern flank of NATO is not new. Nils Orvik, the Norwegian-born director of the Centre of International Relations at Queen's University in Kingston, has long argued that precisely such a necessity exists to defend what he calls the Alliance's "Northern Rim."*

As Canada forms an essential part of the northern region, it would be to the benefit of the western Alliance as well as to Canada's national interests to initiate preparations for the establishment of a system of new NATO bases in the Northern Rim for deterrence as well as defence. Participating in such measures is clearly within the range of Canada's capabilities. It might also satisfy the demands for a higher Canadian content in national defence operations. If we want a more meaningful, identifiable contribution, this may be the best way to do it.

John Gellner, the professional military analyst, has also developed this idea, taking into account the probable ineffectiveness of Canada's NATO commitments in the event of a major crisis.

We can not effectively contribute to deterrence of conventional aggression. In conventional warfare one needs firepower and mass, both from Day One. Losses, especially in material, are bound to be immeasurably higher than in the Second World War. (In the Yom Kippur War, which lasted three weeks, the two sides lost about 1,500 tanks, one every 20 minutes, and about 500 combat aircraft, one every hour.) Under these conditions, there will be no time to raise armies after the outbreak of hostil-

*The only NATO base in the area is at Keflavik in Iceland. Greenland has American air and warning installations at Thule and Sondre Stromfjord. The Faeroe Islands host a NATO base (Morkevik) for warning and communication, but allow no stationing of armed forces. Greenland had a number of major bases during the Second World War, such as the base site at Nassarssuaq, which could be easily reactivated.

ities, as we did in two world wars. The Canadian contribution to conventional deterrence in Europe thus may be politically significant; militarily it is meaningless. There is just no return for the money expended.

On the other hand, we can contribute significantly to nuclear deterrence through control of the strategic forefield (the whole of Canada right to the North Pole) that shields the U.S. nuclear deterrent forces and thus helps make them credible. Here it is the quality of material and personnel which matters, not mass. We should try to concentrate on that. It should be possible to persuade our European allies that in the field of nuclear deterrence we perform an essential function which nobody else can perform, and that our providing that expensive droplet to conventional deterrence in Europe is just a waste of money and effort. This control of the strategic forefield of the nuclear deterrent force protecting the Western alliance . . . goes hand in hand with the general surveillance over our own land, air space and sea approaches. Here, there is still a lot to be done. A small intervention force of all arms, backed by sufficient Reserves, could be kept in hand in Canada for fast action, if and when required.

FEW CANADIANS ARE AWARE that the Soviet threat is no distant, theoretical possibility. No one at Defence Headquarters is willing to discuss the details. But the fact is that between ten and a dozen Soviet submarines are on permanent station in the North Atlantic, lying at the bottom of the ocean, their missiles targeted on American and Canadian cities.* Even with the relatively primitive equipment carried by Canadian ships, destroyer-escorts operating out of Halifax during 1982 made 166 sightings of Soviet submarines. Most belonged to the older Yankee-class, but the brand-new Typhoon-class subs are due to come on station.

The submarines that roost below the ice cap off Labrador are impossible to detect. The differences in temperature of water

---

*On any typical day there are also up to forty-five Soviet fishing trawlers in the waters off Canada's coasts − some of them actually fishing.

layers cause sonar impulses to bounce off each gradient without allowing the undersea vessel to be spotted. Other Soviet subs are known to be hiding near the rusted hulls of merchant ships sunk during the Second World War, so that searching devices dismiss them as recognized and uninteresting echoes. One of the still-secret Canadian espionage cases concerns the transmission to the Soviets of a confidential map showing the locale of these wrecks.

Testifying before a recent Parliamentary Committee on national defence, Captain T. C. Pullen, formerly skipper of HMCS *Labrador*, now a consultant on arctic navigation, described this threat:

> The deep-water route between Ellesmere Island and Greenland affords access to an ideal launch point in northern Baffin Bay in the vicinity of, say, Jones Sound, from which all North American targets within 3,000 nautical miles could be at risk. Targets as close as Ottawa – 1,800 nautical miles – and as far away as San Diego – 2,800 nautical miles; as far east as Halifax or Norfolk, and as far west as Vancouver or San Francisco – are all vulnerable. From such a favourable location, using ice as a shield, one Soviet Typhoon-class submarine could take out most major North American cities. To become aware of such penetrations by submarines which may be bent on deadly mischief, and creeping in on us not only from the Atlantic or the Pacific, but over the roof of America, is one thing, but to be able to do something about it in timely fashion is quite another. An ill-disposed submarine lurking behind a screen of icebergs and under a mantle of sea ice could play a waiting game, keeping thoroughly informed on activities going on all around her, thanks in large measure to the garrulousness of North Americans when they get their hands on a radio. During the Distant Early Warning Line construction in the 1950s, Radio Moscow used to broadcast reports identifying ships, cargoes, tonnages, everything that was going on. Radio discipline in the North was and still remains unbridled.

Paradoxically, but hardly surprisingly, it has been the Americans who have recognized the primary threat to Canada's Arctic. The United States Navy is rushing to completion special submarine designs to hunt and fight Soviet strategic-missile-firing underwater craft, operating below our arctic ice cap. According to Admiral James Watkins, the American Chief of Naval Operations, "We're putting more emphasis on under-ice operations. The Soviets are demonstrating a strong interest in operating under the ice. We'd better be able to know how to fight them in that region." Watkins has referred to the USSR underwater tactics as "a whole new ballgame," indicating that the Soviets are already deploying missile-firing submarines in northern waters with accompanying "attack" subs riding shotgun alongside.

This is only one of the factors transforming our North into a hunk of geography which must be protected. If we value our sovereignty, we cannot request any other power, no matter how friendly, to take over that function for us.

For these and other other reasons Canada must begin to defend her Arctic. Supplementing the refrains of standing on guard for the true North strong and free, Gilles Vigneault's evocative anthem, "*Mon pays . . . c'est l'hiver*" must speak for us all.

CHAPTER SIXTEEN

Defence for the Eighties

At the moment, according to official, if secret, Privy Council documents, defence ranks fourteenth in the Trudeau government's list of operational priorities. That gives the military a lower call on federal funds and energies than fish, convicts, or hog subsidies.

I T IS TIME FOR CANADA to become involved in its own defence. This implies a touch of disassociation in our military relations with the United States. To advocate such a course of action is the rankest of heresies among Canadian defence planners, yet it must be done. Certainly, we should remain in NORAD and NATO, but as ourselves, not as a branch plant of the American military machine.

Not to have an independent defence policy means that we would eventually become one of those wispy client-states that depend on the Pentagon for their very existence. An articulate representative of this point of view – that political freedom requires military independence – was none other than George Washington, who knew something about American politics. Though he was speaking in a different context, the first American president was applying the same logic to his country as we must apply to ours when he declared,

It is folly for one nation to look for disinterested favours from another. It must pay with a proportion of its independence for whatever it may accept under that character. By such acceptance, it may place itself in the condition of having given equivalents for nominal favours, and yet of being reproached with ingratitude for not giving more. There can be no greater error than to expect, or calculate upon, real favours from nation to nation. It is an illusion which experience must cure, which a just pride ought to discard.

CANADA AND THE UNITED STATES have preserved friendly military relations since after the War of 1812, and, in a very real sense, we are the ultimate hostages of the Americans' good intentions. Until the technology of land war is completely transformed, the United States is the only nation that can physically invade Canada.

At the same time, Canada's independence is a perishable commodity: throughout recorded history, any country that has grown totally dependent on another for its self-defence has eventually become that nation's colony.

Most Canadians have managed to develop and maintain a mental dichotomy about American military adventures abroad. Many saw nothing out of the ordinary, for example, about the fact that, during the Vietnam War, Canada was at the same time a major manufacturer of napalm for the U.S. Marine Corps and the chief haven for American deserters and draft dodgers.

Present collective defence arrangements between the two countries date back to 1940 and the formulation by President Franklin Delano Roosevelt and Prime Minister Mackenzie King of the "Ogdensburg Declaration," which established the Canada–United States Permanent Joint Board of Defence. With the mandate to "consider in the broad sense, the defence of the north half of the western hemisphere," the Board and its joint committees began the task of continental defence planning which served as the basis for effective wartime co-operation. It was the first time that the defence of North America had been officially declared, by the leaders of the two countries that divide its real estate, to be a single enterprise.

Since 1945, we have accepted as a principle that no country is capable of providing alone for its own defence and that the only alternative is collective security. Thus we are sheltered beneath the multilateral umbrella of NATO – but more particularly under the protection of the Pentagon.

In the post-war period, the continued existence of the Permanent Joint Board of Defence was affirmed; its planning committees took on a more formal structure in 1946 to become the Canada–United States Military Co-operation Committee. This committee, charged with the task of co-ordinating combined military plans for the defence of North America, is now directly subordinate to the Chiefs of Defence Staff of each country.

When NATO was first formed in 1949, the North Atlantic Council established five NATO regions, with a military planning group for each. In 1950, in response to the increasing threat in Europe, the North Atlantic Council agreed to the formation of allied military commands. Alone of the territories involved in the Alliance, North America was not transformed into such a command because of the undesirable public relations prospect of there being a Supreme Allied Commander, North America, based in Washington.

Instead, Canada and the United States entered into bilateral arrangements to facilitate joint defence activities. These include: a Canada–United States Defence/Production Sharing Agreement, flowing out of the Hyde Park Declaration of 1941; the Canada–United States Civil Emergency Planning Committee; the Canada–United States Inter-Parliamentary Group; the Canada–United States Military Cooperation Committee; and NATO's Regional Planning Group (CUSRPG).

The most significant joint military command was the formation of NORAD. The North American Air Defence Command was made responsible to the Canadian Chiefs of Staff Committee (later the Chief of the Defence Staff) and to the United States Joint Chiefs of Staff, for the continent's air defence.

Through the daily functioning of NORAD and NATO, Canadian military strategists by necessity have had to plan for the defence of the whole of the North American sub-continent rather than of the two countries that share it. In the process, the forty-ninth parallel, which divides Canada from the United States, has frequently been reduced in importance, considered as nothing more than a latitudinal line on the map, like the equator or the Arctic Circle. During the 1950s and well into the 1960s, this attitude was characterized by General Charles Foulkes, then Chairman of the Canadian Chiefs of Staff, who talked glowingly about relying on "Brad" and "Rad" (the American army's General Bradley and navy's Admiral

Radford) at the Pentagon to pass on through the "old boy net-work" strictly confidential but adaptable hints about how Canada should be planning its defences. George Ignatieff, then an Assistant Secretary of State for External Affairs in Ottawa, later noted that when the Liberal government of Louis St. Laurent ordered the setting-up of a joint committee to study the defence implications of the missile age and asked General Foulkes to share his information, "these appeals were studiously ignored by General Foulkes on the grounds that it might cut off USA intelligence if 'eggheads' from External Affairs were allowed to share confidential advice received from the Pentagon."

FOULKES WAS WRONG THEN and such policies would be wrong now. The Cold War has always suffered from mutually reinforcing misconceptions, fed by Soviet ignorance of American intentions – and vice versa – with both superpowers being guilty of perpetuating outdated stereotypes of each other. One problem with superpowers is that their leaders tend to view the world in evangelical terms, believing in the uniqueness of their mission, continually asking themselves whether they are still Number One. The consequence of such *hubris* is an often mindless quest for military superiority.

Canada has been a part of this deadly contest.

We are, by geography and by choice, firmly tied into the North Atlantic Treaty Organization, which, despite its weaknesses and contradictions, has managed to maintain a semblance of peace for more than three decades.

It is the multilateral nature of that Alliance that must be stressed in our future planning, rather than the expansion of bilateral relations with the United States. A recent study endorsed by the Atlantic Council of Canada, after analyzing contemporary American foreign policies, noted that:

The multifarious motivations of the actors, the intensity of the pressures to which an Administration is subjected, the bizarre linkages and confusion of issues that often result, create a dangerous potential for irrational action. The development of a

164

certain strategic weapon, for example, may become so much identified with the maintenance of American political will that all the sound arguments marshalled against it are to no avail, while an arms limitation agreement may be debated in terms that have much more to do with domestic politics than with the substance of the treaty. In such circumstances, the forces favorable to a Canadian viewpoint are sure to need bolstering, and only a public expression of views will have any effect. That this will create difficulties for the tactical management of Canada's relations with the United States is undeniable, but it is not foreordained that the two governments will invariably be at odds, and there will still be plenty of scope for co-operative words and actions, judiciously employed, to temper any resentment occasioned by Canada's more outspoken attitude.

On the other hand, Edward Littwak of Georgetown University's Center for Strategic and International Studies and a member of Ronald Reagan's defence transition team, told *Maclean's*:

Canada is a country that has decided to take a free ride. It has historically gotten away with it and wants to continue getting away with it. The Administration has a real problem here. If we hector and lecture, then everybody will say that it's counterproductive. They will say that it merely irritates, stimulates nationalism and backlash, and so on. If we don't say anything, then the Canadians are allowed to comfortably forget all about the problem. It's something for the Canadian elite to contend with. Are they comfortable in this posture of being essentially irresponsible children in the alliance? If they want to go on in this lukewarm, comfortable pool, that's fine − but please don't ask people to treat Canada as an equal and as a partner and as an ally, because it is not an equal and a partner and an ally.

Mr. Littwak notwithstanding, we must start moving out from the shadow of *Pax Americana* as soon as possible, disassociating ourselves more forcefully from Washington's international initiatives, including its newest adventures south of the Rio Grande and in Africa. As Nicholas von Hoffman, the American political commentator recently noted: "The United States has more nuclear aircraft carriers than it has citizens who can tell whether Chad is a nation, a fish, or the name of a rock band. Almost every morning an armada of ghastly power has been dispatched to some other place in which only the ideological fanatics in the Administration are interested."

The problem with American defence policy – apart from its regional territorial ambitions – is that so many of the Pentagon's decisions are postures not adequately thought through. As James Fallows, the *Atlantic Monthly*'s former Washington editor has noted, national defence policy in the United States is so borne away by theory that it loses touch with facts, historical experience, and simple common sense. The Pentagon's positions are all too reminiscent of the third and least known of Gulliver's travels, when Gulliver visits the Kingdom of Laputa. There he finds a nation given over to philosophical speculations and "pure reason," rather than common sense. Its citizens have ill-fitting clothes because they are designed with compass and quadrant rather than being measured for the wearer. The kingdom's houses are in disrepair because tradesmen are more interested in drawing fancy designs than erecting sound structures. "In political arguments about defense," Fallows pointed out,

> there is a Laputan tendency to stick to the plane of generalization, rather than concentrating on detailed, case-by-case assessments of the facts. When public discussions about defense move away from the specifics, their real subject usually becomes something other than defense itelf. They may be displays of right- and left-wing ideologies; they may be tests of "hard" and "soft" philosophies of international relations. They may even be proxies for whether one was raised as a child to consider the world hostile or benign. Most often, they collapse into the familiar choice between "more" and "less" defense, measured solely by money spent and programs begun. For partisans of "strength" and "restraint" alike, the unspoken assumption has been that what finally matters in defense is the overall budget figure. To those who favor "more defense," a dollar spent on one weapon is about as good as a dollar spent on another. Those who call for "reordering national priorities" or an end to the

arms race are rarely heard supporting any weapon at all. Both sides suffer from the ancient fallacy of measuring input, rather than output – judging how hard you try, rather than what you accomplish. Neither goes far toward ensuring that items that would come first, second, third, on any rational list of what the nation needs for defense are the ones we end up having.

THE FIRST AND MOST IMPORTANT STEP in reclaiming independence for Canada's armed forces is that they be officially denuclearized. We don't need nuclear warheads for any of our weapons and we should publicly reject, once and for all, their use by our troops, planes, and warships. We were the first country with the capacity to produce nuclear weapons which deliberately chose not to do so. We are also the only nuclear-armed nation which has opted to divest itself of nuclear weapons. We must not acquire them again.

As founding members of NATO, we cannot escape bearing our share of the responsibility inherent in the Alliance's maintenance of a credible nuclear deterrent. But the fact that both our political and military leaders have jettisoned nuclear warheads as indigenous weapons; the fact that we have not, for more than a decade, permitted exports of Canadian uranium to be used for military purposes; and the fact that we have a tradition of peace-keeping and a stance of non-aggression vis-a-vis other countries – these should become the elements of a new defence policy.

We should publicly declare ourselves to be a non-nuclear member of the NATO Alliance, bound to its overall strategy but determinedly refusing to adopt any nuclear warheads for our own use. While fully recognizing that this leaves aside the moral dilemma of depending for our security on an Alliance still heavily bound to its nuclear deterrent, it is a step worth taking.

But it cannot be taken in isolation. To make our stance credible, such a declaration must be accompanied by the quantity and quality of expansion in our *conventional* military capabilities as outlined in these pages. By strengthening our conventional forces – even though we reject any nuclear role – our international credibility will be maintained.

To give our military a significant function of its own, Ottawa should consider establishing a new Northern Command for NATO, incorporating a rejuvenated and adequately financed Canadian navy, army, and air force. The Soviets are using the Arctic as one of their most vital strategic areas of operation. Murmansk is the main holding pen for Soviet ballistic missile-carrying submarines. The Russians deploy a large fleet of powerful icebreakers, including the *Sibir* and the *Arktik* (the first ship ever to ram her way to the North Pole) and have many shallow-draught breakers that command the northern sea routes. They enjoy *de facto* control of the Arctic Ocean.

If our defence efforts were aimed at protecting the Arctic Circle, Canada could make a realistic contribution to NATO's credibility. At the same time we could strengthen claims on our own sovereignty in the North with its vast potential oil wealth.

One minor but useful immediate diplomatic initiative would be to open a Canadian embassy at Reykjavik, Iceland. It is the capital of an allied, northern, strategically vital and politically vulnerable island-nation which has a substantial immigrant population in Canada. It is no accident that the USSR has an embassy in Reykjavik which houses more than two hundred diplomats (Iceland itself has a population of less than 225,000). Translating that ratio to Canada would mean that the Soviet Embassy in Ottawa would have a staff of twenty thousand.

Some of the more urgent defence requirements described previously include:

- The purchase of a wing of AWACS for northern Canadian surveillance.
- De-unification of the armed forces.
- Strengthening of the Canadian navy, Coast Guard, and merchant marine.
- A decisive tilting of the centre of gravity of our defence structure westward in the recognition of our growing status as a Pacific Rim nation.
- The dropping of our NATO commitment to Norway which we could not, in any realistic way, hope to meet. At the same time, we should bring home all of the CF-18s for domestic defence.

There are many, relatively inexpensive ways to increase the

effectiveness of back-up forces. Every pilot in Air India, for example, is a reserve officer in the Indian Air Force. None of our merchant ships' crews have had any training that would prepare them to provide the kind of aid that allowed Britain to stage its successful supply operation for the Falklands campaign.

The number of extra reservists required to bring the Canadian forces up to par is about eighty-five thousand. It would be reasonable to expect that such an addition might result after about five years of an expanded, voluntary program. Enlistment should be encouraged by having reservists' earnings made tax-free – a provision already enacted in Australia. At the same time, the reserves in all three services should have their equipment brought up to par with their regular brethren-in-arms – since they would be assigned to use similar hardware in the event of any emergency. Officer training schemes should be revived at Canadian universities, with initial concentration on the twelve Canadian institutions of higher learning currently teaching courses in strategic studies. Many more scholarships should be offered at the Royal Military College, Kingston; le Collège militaire royal, Saint-Jean; and Royal Roads Military College, Victoria.

The capital-expenditures side of the ledger must be doubled annually (in real terms) over the next decade to yield an extra $2 billion. In other words, the existing defence budget should be increased to 3.6 per cent of the GNP – hardly an unattainable ideal. That would be enough to renew the defence department's basic equipment every twenty years.

My recommendation that Canada's defence budget be doubled may seem like an irresponsible suggestion at a time when government expenditures are being reduced in other sectors. But no industrialized nation devotes less of its resources to defence than does Canada, even though the social and economic pressures that exist in this country are not that different from similar problems in other democracies. Every recommendation in this book for a more meaningful *Canadian* defence could be realized by moving our military budget to 3.6 per cent of our gross national product. This would put us on a par with other, decidedly unwarlike countries, such as Sweden (3.1%), the Netherlands (3.4%) and Australia (3%). As the Senate's Standing Committee on Foreign Affairs noted recently: "The current Canadian level of expenditures on defence does little more than buy the country the worst of both worlds. While the expenditures are large enough to represent a significant charge on the national exchequer, they are too small to produce worthwhile results."

One highly controversial method of getting more defence per dollar spent would be either to purchase some of our large units abroad ("off-the-shelf") or, even better, to manufacture ships, aircraft, and other units in Canada that could be sold abroad. "One can imagine," wrote John D. Harbron, foreign news analyst for Thomson Newspapers,

> the private flap which would take place in federal cabinets, as presently constituted, and the public outburst which would take place if we succeeded, say, in selling a small class of multi-purpose frigates to Argentina, which in effect, we tried to do in 1970. Yet, if we had won that contract, which went to the much more aggressive British, it would have supplied us with the state-of-the-art to build our own fleet of mixed purpose naval ships, with air capability for both sovereignty surveillance and [anti-submarine warfare] activities, a type and kind of warship we are not going to build – even now . . . . One wonders if the Italian shipbuilding industry, which has established one of the most aggressive small warship building and export programs in NATO, could build our frigates sooner and better than our own industry.

Harbron has also touched on that most sensitive of Canadian defence issues: the fact that we have no mobilization plan. "Though the Department of National Defence denies it," Harbron noted, ". . . its senior military management is inhibited from drawing up such a plan by federal cabinets with ministers who reject it as basically 'sinister' and [who are] supported by a massively negative and often severely mis-informed public opinion that preparation for conflict is 'immoral.'"

WHEN ANDRÉ LAURENDEAU, then editor of *Le Devoir*, first

proposed a national inquiry into the state of bilingualism in Canada, he ventured to suggest: "If Paris was worth a mass, Canada is worth a royal commission."

We tend to study our problems intead of resolving them, and one more drawn-out investigation of our defence problems would add little to the sum of universal knowledge. Yet Canada's current military priorities remain based on a White Paper written more than a dozen years ago. Titled *Defence in the 1970s*, the document was little more than a motherhood endorsement of Canada's defence function as being:

- the protection of our sovereignty;
- the defence of North America in co-operation with the United States;
- the fulfilment of NATO commitments;
- international peacekeeping.

This outdated paper fails to take into account the new strategic environment in which we find ourselves.

A new White Paper* is urgently required to determine the policies we should follow in formulating a plausible *Defence for the 1980s*.

At the same time, instead of attempting to detour the popular feeling for disarmament, the government should seize the opportunity to become much more active in world organizations dedicated to the issue. This would include:

- participating more actively in the Vienna negotiations on Mutual and Balanced Force Reductions (MBFR);
- doing its utmost to promote the establishment of early agreements and investing more effort and technical expertise in this issue, as necessary;
- financing our scientists to work co-operatively in the area of arms control and disarmament verification;
- demanding an early resumption of strategic arms limitation and reduction talks (formerly SALT, now START) with strict deadlines;

*A White Paper is a statement of government policy; a Green Paper is a discussion document.

- clearly endorsing the Anti-Ballistic Missile (ABM) Treaty;
- campaigning for a multilateral Comprehensive Test Ban at the earliest possible time;
- exhorting all nations to adhere to the 1975 convention on the prohibition of the development, production, and stockpiling of bacteriological (biological) and toxic weapons;
- confirming Canada's support for other limited arms control agreements such as the Seabed Arms Control Treaty of 1972 and the environmental modification conventions of 1977 and of 1981 banning the use of those conventional weapons considered to be excessively inhumane or indiscriminate;
- endorsing the new agreements which would reinforce the 1967 Outer Space Treaty by prohibiting the development, testing, or deployment of all weapons;
- supporting the establishment of an International Satellite Monitoring Agency.

CANADIANS PRIDE THEMSELVES in regarding war as an aberration – a last resort to be abominated and deplored.

It is all that and more. But the threat to our "peaceable kingdom" is very real. Ignoring it won't make it vanish.

Our armed forces may justifiably be painted as having become inefficient and even irrelevant. But their inadequacies are due not to their lack of professionalism. Even in their present sorry state, unit for unit, aircraft for aircraft, and ship for ship, they do as well, and usually better than most other NATO elements. For the most part, our military are honourable and intelligent men and women who have given their country more defence than its dollars deserved to buy.

It is time to redress the balance.

We are a liberal democracy with no imperialistic ambitions. Our military minds suffer from no delusions of grandeur and few mercenary impulses. Our defence planners have been the victims of short-sighted politicians, so anxious to get themselves re-elected that they have forgotten that the real purpose of their mandate is to lead, not follow, public opinion.

National defence must become a priority concern of our political leaders, and not just a bothersome afterthought. The development of a national will and the creation among Canadian voters of an understanding of what it takes to survive in this dangerous age is an issue which deserves to be placed at the top of any realistic political agenda for the 1980s.

At the moment, according to official, if secret, Privy Council documents, defence ranks fourteenth in the Trudeau government's list of operational priorities. That gives the military a lower call on federal funds and energies than fish, convicts, or hog subsidies.

Canadians must take stock of themselves and their country and decide, once and for all, whether to assert that we are a sovereign state, or to continue being a wholly dependent colony, owing our safety and continued existence to the tender mercies of the Pentagon.

Armies mirror the characteristics of the societies on whose behalf they fight, whether they be instruments of freedom and liberation or of repression and tyranny. Our defence forces, such as they are, exist to safeguard the interests of Canadian society, and if their ultimate role seems hard to pin down, it's because we, as a people, lack a definable creed or even a set of common beliefs.

But in the final analysis, our survival on this delicate planet hinges on our will to protect our institutions, and that, in turn, depends on how much we learn to value them.

AWACS	Airborne Warning and Control System. Large, long-endurance transport-type aircraft fitted with high-powered surveillance and control radars and extensive communications. A crew of controllers and radar operators can detect enemy aircraft and direct fighter and missile attacks against them.
BMD	Ballistic Missile Defence.
BMEWS	Ballistic Missile Early Warning System. Three powerful, computer-assisted radars, located in Alaska, Greenland, and England, which can detect and predict the flight of ICBMs aimed at North America. The data from the stations is sent to the main defence computer at NORAD Headquarters.
Bomarc	A ground-to-air anti-aircraft missile which is no longer operational.
Brigade Group	An autonomous land-force formation of less than divisional strength with its own armour, artillery, signals, and supporting arms.
B-52	An eight-engined jet bomber built by Boeing Aircraft Corp., operational since the late 1950s.
CAST	Canadian Air-Sea Transportable Brigade Group. A force normally stationed in Canada which will be air- and sea-lifted to Norway in case of hostilities.

Cold War	Conflict carried out by overt and covert methods without recourse to military confrontation. Specifically, the ongoing hostility between the West and Russia.
Congress of Vienna	A conference called by the victorious allies in 1814 after Napoleon's abdication and his banishment to Elba. The Congress tried to settle the numerous territorial claims and was still in session when Napoleon escaped from Elba.
COTC	See ROTP
Cryogenics	A branch of science concerned with the use and effects of very low temperatures.
C-5	Lockheed Galaxy. Probably the largest military logistic transport aircraft in the world, it can carry two M-60 tanks or sixteen three-quarter-ton trucks plus 75 fully armed troops. As a troop carrier it can carry 345 troops with their light support equipment. (Not to be confused with the Canadair C-5. Only one of these was built as a VIP transport in the 1950s. It served until 1968).
CF-5	The Canadian version of the Northrop F-5 series light tactical ground support fighter. In different versions served in the air forces of at least twenty-two countries. This aircraft was able to carry a variety of weapon loads so was extremely versatile.

CF-18   The McDonnell-Douglas Hornet fighter air-
                  craft presently being procured by the Canadian
                  air element.

CF-101   The Voodoo, designed and built in the US as
                  the F-101 in 1964 and later built in Canada. It is
                  still in use but will be replaced by the CF-18.

CF-104   The Starfighter, a 1966 vintage attack aircraft
                  now in service only in Canada and Turkey.

DEW Line   Distant Early Warning Line. An Arctic radar
                  chain stretching from Alaska to Greenland.
                  There are four stations in the Canadian Arctic.

Dakota   The C-47 twin-propellor transport aircraft. A
                  military version of the Douglas DC-3 which
                  served through the Second World War and is
                  still in military and commercial service.

END   European Nuclear Disarmament Movement.

Exocet   A French-designed and -built air-to-ground
                  laser-guided missile which had some success
                  against the Royal Navy in the Falklands War.

FNC   A Belgian-designed 7.62mm rifle which was
                  accepted as the standard NATO infantry weapon
                  in the 1960s and is still in common use.

FLQ	*Front de Liberation du Québec.* A political group dedicated to obtaining Quebec sovereignty, by force if necessary.
ICBM	Inter-Continental Ballistic Missile.
IRA	Irish Republican Army. An illegal para-military organization dedicated to uniting Northern Ireland and Eire by terrorist methods.
KGB	*Komitet Gosudarstovennoi Bezopastnosti* – Soviet State Security Committee. The Russian Secret Service.
Kiloton	An explosive force equivalent to that of 1000 tons of TNT.
MBFR	Mutual and Balanced Force Reductions. Part of the SALT talks in Vienna.
Mid-Canada Line	A chain of fixed, unattended Doppler radars across Canada to detect all air movements. Unfortunately this included the flight of migrating birds so the line was never successful and was dismantled more than a decade ago.
MIRV	Multiple Independently Targetable Re-entry Vehicle. The Soviet SS-20 is a MIRV.
NATO	North Atlantic Treaty Organization.

NORAD	North American Air Defence Command when formed in 1958. After the headquarters were moved under Cheyenne Mountain, near Colorado Springs and surveillance of space became important, the name was changed to North American Aerospace Defence Command.
PARS	Phased Array Radar System. A high-powered radar which has a very large fixed antenna array. The elements of the array are switched (phase-changed) to produce moving radar beams.
Pinetree Line	A system of manned radars across the southern part of Canada. The radars provide data for surveillance of unidentified aircraft and control of fighters.
ROTP	Regular Officers Training Plan (successor of the Canadian Officers Training Corps). A university cadet organization which subsidized the tuition of undergraduates who took military training both part-time during the academic year and full-time with the regular service during the summer.
SALT-I	Strategic Arms Limitation Treaty-I between the United States and the Soviet Union was ratified in 1972. A subsequent treaty, SALT-II, has not been ratified by the United States.
SSN-2	Styx. A Soviet ship-to-ship missile which was used successfully by the Egyptian navy in attacks against Israeli naval vessels.

SS-20   The Soviet medium-range ballistic missile.

TERCOM   An electronic terrain guidance system used in
                 the US cruise missile. The contours of the
                 ground en route to the target are programmed
                 into a radar guidance system.

VHF   Very High Frequency. Frequencies in the 30
                 MegaHertz to 300 MegaHertz region.

Warsaw Pact   The Eastern bloc's response to NATO. A military
                 mutual aggression pact between USSR and her
                 satellite states.

Index

183